Y0-CAR-647

This Could Be Us But You Playin'

By:
Cachet

DOUGLASS BRANCH LIBRARY
Champaign Public Library
504 East Grove Street
Champaign, Illinois 61820-3239

This Could Be Us But You Playin'

©Copyright 2016 Cachet

Published by:
Cole Hart Presents

All rights reserved. No part of this book may be used or reproduced in any manner whatsoever without written permission from the publisher, except where permitted by law.

This is a work of fiction. Any resemblance to actual persons living or dead is purely coincidental.

First Trade Paperback Edition Printing 2016

ISBN-13: 978-1523498383
ISBN-10: 1523498382

Dedication

This book is dedicated to my husband, Stephen Andres Sr., and my children; Keiasya, Tre'Maine, Stephen Jr., and Zaria. Thank you all for letting me experience the kind of love that many people would die for.

To everyone who has ever picked up a book with Cachet on the cover.

My stories would go unread if it wasn't for all of you.
It's your support that keeps me doing what I do.
I appreciate you guys more than you'll ever know.
So please stick around and watch as I continue to grow.
As an author, storyteller, or writer, which ever you choose,
And know that I read each and every one of your reviews.

So thank you again, for your love and support,
And know that I'll try my best to never fall short.

 ***♥♥♥ Cachet ♥♥♥***

Author Contact:

Email: AuthorCachet@gmail.com

Facebook: Cachet Andres

Instagram: __Cachet__

Twitter: CachetNicole

The course of true love never did run smooth.

~William Shakespeare~

Prologue

Kaleb looked down at his phone as he used his thumb to scroll down the many pictures that had been posted. There were quite a few selfies, photos of little kids dressed as grown-ups and more memes than he could keep up with. Kaleb paused for a second when he came across one picture that stood out. It was a plate of food. A quick glance at the poster's name forced him to chuckle out loud. With a name like *'TightN'JuicyKat'*, he hoped that her box was good and wet like she claimed because from the photo that he was looking at, she damn sure couldn't cook if her life depended on it. The fact that she posted it made him wonder what the hell she was thinking in the first place.

The plate that was sloppily made looked disgusting and just the thought of eating something so vile made him sick to his stomach. There were three pieces of fried chicken legs that were doused with hot sauce, but even then, Kaleb could still see that they were way too dark for his liking. To the left of the chicken was a clump of extremely soupy macaroni and to the right sat a pile of collard greens that were stiff looking. They also looked like the chick had just pulled them off the stem a few minutes prior because they didn't looked to be cooked at all. The very last thing he saw on the dish made Kaleb do a double take. It was a charred slice of cornbread that she had the nerve to put a large piece of butter on top of, as if that would actually help.

"I hope this shit is a fucking joke," he said to himself in utter disgust.

"Nah, this ain't no joke, mu'fucka. This ass whipping you getting in pool is for real, nigga," Desmond, his best friend, teased as he sunk another ball into the pocket. "I want my damn money too, and I don't wanna hear no shit about paying me later. Cash out is today."

"Man, ain't nobody thinking about yo' old non-shooting ass." Kaleb laughed as he shot a quick glance toward the pool table before returning his focus back to his phone.

It was a Friday night and since it had been raining since earlier, the two best friends were in the basement of Kaleb's home drinking and playing a few games of pool. When Desmond saw what his friend was doing, he snorted.

"I should've known yo' ass was over there on Instagram. Don't you ever get tired of that fake shit?" Desmond asked as he bent down and lined up to take his next shot.

"What's fake about it?" Kaleb asked. He already knew the answer to his question; he just liked to see his boy riled up.

"Nigga, are you serious?" Desmond asked, taking the bait after he sunk yet another shot. He laid the pool stick on the table and walked over to where Kaleb was sitting, before he broke down his logic. "Everything is fake about that bullshit. First, you got those cement booty ass *models,* who swear they the shit because they got a few thousand followers. For some reason, they don't understand that the only reason niggas are on their pages is because they are always posting damn near naked pictures. Hoes got booking info in their bio,

~ 3 ~

but the only places you ever see 'em is on IG or in some smoky ass club. What I don't understand is how does having fifty thousand followers and posting butt shots all day qualify you as a model?" Desmond asked, even though he wasn't looking for an answer. "Then, you got the *ballers*, who are always posting pictures of money and what they got. See them niggas out and about in real life, and they begging you to either pay their way in the club or buy 'em a drink." Desmond shook his head. "Broke niggas flexing for the gram."

"I know a few of them," Kaleb agreed.

"Then it's the *miserable* chicks."

"Who?"

"Yeah, you know who I'm talking about. Those are the ones who are always male bashing, posting those corny ass quotes all the time. Either her man left her for another bitch, or he's cheating on her ass every chance he gets. Whichever the reason that fits is why she's always mad and talking shit. It's because she's miserable."

Kaleb laughed. "Who the fuck you think you are, some kind of psychiatrist or something? You breaking shit down like you know these folks or something."

"Shit, I might as well because their stories are always the same. I know how people work bro." Desmond smiled cockily as he took a seat on the bar stool beside his friend. "What about the *happily single* chicks? Always posting shit about the single life. They are quick to claim independent and are always buying themselves shit just to post it, knowing they wish they had a nigga to do the shit for them. That or at least to dick them down every once in a while because some of these hoes so backed up; I know for a fact that a lil' piece of dick would have them cool, calm, and collective." He rubbed his hand across his face, while he cracked up at his own joke. Once he finished chuckling, he continued.

"Let's not forget the chick who swears that she has the best man in the world. She uploads a hundred pictures of them doing dumb shit like watching TV, sleeping, or eating. There are a million screenshots posted of all of the cute and loving things he says. This is all so she can show the world that she got a man. Never once does the bitch post of picture of them going out. You wanna know why?"

"I'm almost afraid to ask," Kaleb sighed.

"Because that nigga either broke as fuck and can't afford to take her ass anywhere, or he don't wanna be seen out in public with her ass because he's embarrassed. That or got another girl. I could go on and on about this subject if you want me to."

"Nigga, shut the fuck up!" Kaleb cracked up. "You always talking shit."

"You know I'm telling the truth though." Desmond laughed. "That's why I ain't on that bullshit no more. I got tired of trying to cypher between what's real and what's fake. I almost got got by a bitch not too long ago. Somehow, this chick ended up following me. Every time I turned around, she was commenting on my pictures with heart emojis and shit like that. One day, for the hell of it, I clicked on her name, and when I did, I seen that she's fine than a muthafucka. I'm talking about this bitch was stacked!" Desmond exclaimed.

"Anyway, we ended up talking. She sending me all kinds of pictures of her and shit. I noticed that even while she's telling me that she's lying down, the pictures she's sending me are always her out and about. So, I ask the hoe to FaceTime me, so I can see her in person. You know, see what she really look like. Man, this hoe gave me every excuse in the book of why we couldn't do it. First her camera was broke, and then her internet was acting up. After a while, I got tired of asking and told her to lose my fucking number because I ain't have time for that catfishing shit. That's when I realized that people can be anyone they wanna be on social media, and I ain't got time to figure out who is who. I got better shit to do with my time."

Desmond picked up his beer that was sitting on top of the bar and took a long swig. When his thirst was quenched, he put the bottle back down and looked over at Kaleb. When he saw him staring intently at something on his phone, he leaned in to see what had his attention.

"Check this shit out right here." Kaleb tilted his phone so that he could get a better look.

"What the fuck is that?" Desmond paused. Once he was sure of what he was seeing, he spoke, "A side nigga contract?" he asked with his eyebrows raised. When he was finished reading it to the end, he chuckled. "People come up with anything these days."

"Hell yeah!" Kaleb agreed. "That shit say, I will be available for you five nights a week, and I will keep my mouth shut about our business at all times," he snorted.

"Yeah, I saw some shit similar to that a little while ago. I started to send it to you, but I figured you had already filled out yours," Desmond said seriously.

"What?" Kaleb looked at him like he was crazy. "Nigga, what the fuck you talking about?"

"I'm talking about the fact that you are Nikki's side nigga?"

"No the fuck I ain't!" Kaleb responded with his face turned up. "We just be fucking around."

"Yeah...a'ight." Desmond dismissed him with a wave of the hand.

"I'm serious, we just be fucking around. She gotta nigga and I'm cool with that."

"Mu'fucka, that is the definition of a side nigga with yo' crazy ass!" Desmond cackled, slapping his hand on top of the bar. He was laughing so hard; he almost fell off the stool.

"See, you tryna play me. You act like I ain't with Te-Te," Kaleb stated, talking about his girlfriend Tiera. "Have you forgot about her?"

"Nigga, have you forgot about her? When was the last time that you took the girl somewhere?" When

Kaleb didn't respond, Desmond continued. "Come on man, you know that I love Te-Te like a sister, but you'd be lying if you said that you wouldn't drop her ass in a split second if Nikki told you that she was ready to be with you and only you." He paused to let his statement marinate. "My question is; do you think she would do the same with her nigga if you told her that you wanted to be exclusive?"

"Hell yeah, I know she would," Kaleb professed, sitting straight up.

"Alright, well in that case, keep doing your thing. Don't let me rain on yo' parade," Desmond said with his hands up in surrender. He stood up and grabbed his jacket off the back of the nearby chair. "Put ya chest in nigga." He laughed. "Got that bitch all poked out like you was ready to do something."

"Fuck you nigga, with yo' yellow ass," Kaleb joked.

"This coming from a mu'fucka that's only a shade darker than me...if that." Desmond paused, shaking his head. "Nah, for real, I just don't want to see you get into trouble behind this shit. Or even worse...hurt."

"I'm good bro," Kaleb assured him, giving his friend a pound.

"Cool because you know I'm behind you no matter what. Right or wrong, I'll fuck something up if I have to," Desmond told him confidently. "That nigga big as shit though, so I'll have to break him down a little bit, but I'll get him together for ya bro," he joked, even though he was dead serious.

"I know you will, and you already know that I'll do the same for you."

"No doubt." Desmond leaned in and pulled his friend into a brotherly hug. "I'll holler at you later, bro."

"Bet."

As Desmond walked away, Kaleb watched him until he rounded the corner and jogged up the stairs. Once his best friend was out of his sight, he sighed and dropped his head. He couldn't help but to think about what Desmond had asked him. Although he claimed that he knew Dominique would leave her dude for him, he was lying. What he didn't tell Desmond was that he had asked her over and again and still, she wouldn't budge. The truth was that Dominique didn't have plans to leave her man alone, even though shit had gotten serious between the two of them. He loved Dominique; always have and probably always would. He just wished that things were different than what they were between them.

Kaleb knew that he was the reason why they weren't together, and it was all because of his fuck up years prior. He realized that there was nothing he could do to change that, even though he would give anything to go back and make it right. Dominique was supposed to be his girl. She was supposed to have bared his children, but instead, she was engaged to be married to someone else. Someone who Kaleb knew was a piece of shit liar who didn't deserve to be anywhere near her. He wasn't a hater though, and didn't voice the things that he knew about her fiancé; who, unbeknownst to Dominique, was grimy as hell and Kaleb knew that for a fact. So, instead of running his mouth like a female, he sat back and hoped that Dominique would see everything for herself. Once that happened, she would run right to him where she should have been from day one.

After sitting in the same spot for a few more minutes, Kaleb got up and headed upstairs. As he grabbed another beer out of the fridge, he came to the conclusion that Dominique was going to have to make up her mind on who she wanted to be with. Kaleb just hoped it was him that she chose because he didn't know what he would do if it wasn't. He was tired of playing the back and forth game with her. One minute, she claimed to be all in, and the next, she was running back to her man. Either she was going to be his and only his, or they were going to have to call it quits. What he didn't know was that either way, it wasn't going to be as easy as he thought that it would be.

Chapter One

Five years earlier...

"Nikki, get yo' ass in here right now and clean up this muthafucking mess!" Monique ordered as she stood in the middle of her kitchen in disbelief. "Nikki!" she yelled out again when she didn't receive an answer.

Her nose flared as she looked at all the messy milk filled bowls that were strewn all over her table. The kitchen chairs, which should have been pushed back in place, were instead scattered about; one even flipped sideways and resting on the floor. Monique's blood boiled when she saw the empty box of Cocoa Puffs as it laid on its side; the chocolatey sugar from the bottom of the bag spilled everywhere. Her daughter had lost her fucking mind if she thought she wasn't going to get her ass beat behind this. Monique had spent the last few hours with her guy friend and was not in the mood for all of the shit that was in front of her. After the rough night she had, her only plan was to come home, take a hot bath, and go to bed. Unfortunately, her relaxing would have to wait because she now had an ass to kick.

Sliding her shoes off, Monique picked them up and shuffled into her bedroom, which was off of the kitchen. After slipping her dress over her shoulders and down her body, she kicked it across the room toward her dirty clothes hamper that sat in the corner. A pile of her previously discarded clothes spilled from the top of the basket and onto the floor. When she noticed them, she turned her nose up. *Nikki's hardheaded ass better make sure that she gets in here to clean my fucking room and wash my clothes tomorrow*, she thought to herself. Taking her focus off of the clothes, Monique opened up the top drawer to her dresser and pulled out a nightshirt. After she slid it over her head and down her naked body, she stepped into her house shoes that were nearby.

As she stood in front of her dresser, Monique took a close look at her face. She turned her head from side to side. She was looking for any scars that may have been present. When she saw a few scratches near her forehead, she pursed her lips before moving her attention to her left eye, which was now swollen and red. Other than those obvious marks, everything else was okay. Thinking about the events from the last hour caused Monique to laugh out loud. Although there was nothing funny at all about the situation, what else could she do to keep herself from crying? Monique couldn't believe how her guy friend had played her and promised herself to tell him exactly how she felt the next time he decided to call her phone, not that she thought he would actually reach out to her after what had gone down at his place.

When Monique finished giving her face another once over, she turned and exited her bedroom. Quickly, she marched down the hall headed to the area where her oldest two daughters slept. As soon as she got to the door, she pushed it open and clicked on the light. On one side of the room was Tiffany, her second oldest daughter. Her hot pink comforter was pulled over her head, and she snored lightly. On the other side of the room was her daughter, Dominque, who was sixteen.

She was laid in her bed sleeping, as if she didn't have a care in the world. This angered Monique because there she was, knocked out in dream land, while her house was a fucking mess.

When Monique left out earlier, she told Dominique to feed the kids, take them a bath, and clean up her house once she was finished, before putting them to bed. This was something that Dominique was responsible for daily, so there was really no need for Monique to explain it to her, even though she did. Apparently, Dominique thought that tonight would be the night that she would say fuck her mother and do what the hell she wanted to do. She was about to soon find out that today was not her lucky day because her mother was in a very foul mood.

"Get the fuck up!" Monique yelled, before she smacked the sleeping teen so hard on the side of the head, it echoed throughout the room.

"Oww!" Dominique howled as she sat up quickly. Her hand rested on the spot where her mother had just struck her.

"What the hell did I tell you to do before I left earlier today?"

The sound of yelling caused Tiffany to stir. She rolled over in her bed and when she did, she caught a glimpse of her mother standing over her sister angrily. Tiffany quickly pulled her covers up over her head and pretended as if she was still sleeping. She knew that if her mother was mad enough to storm into their room in the middle of the night, she was pissed. There was no doubt in Tiffany's mind why her mother was upset. She knew that it was because of the mess in the kitchen. Before they went to bed, Tiffany started to remind Dominique about cleaning it, but when she saw just how tired her sister was, she decided not to mention it. In the back of Tiffany's mind, she believed that maybe her mother wouldn't come home that night, so her and Dominique would have a chance to clean up before they headed off to school. Seeing her mother now, standing there livid, made her wish that she had just spoke up.

"I don't remember!" Dominique snapped, still holding on to where she had been hit.

It wasn't that she was trying to get smart with her mother, it just happened to come out that way. Truthfully, Dominique was confused by what was going on. After being woke up from her sleep with a hit to the head, she didn't have a clue what her mother was talking about. Before she had a chance to really think about what the problem was, Monique was hitting her once again, this time with a closed fist. Dominique's head jerked back violently and bounced off the wall. She instantly saw stars. The pain in the back of her head throbbed and the aching in her eye made her say a silent prayer that it wouldn't be black the next day. If so, Dominque knew that she was going to have to figure out a way to cover it. Being at school with a shiner from her mother the next day weighted heavy on her mind for a split second, before she was brought back out of her thoughts.

"Who the fuck you talking to like that, bitch?" Monique asked with her head cocked to the side and her hands balled into fist. She didn't give Dominique a chance to explain herself before she punched her again, this time, square in the nose.

The fact that she thought that her daughter had gotten smart made Monique upset, but not enough to do what she was doing at the present time. No, Monique was pissed about what had gone down earlier with her guy friend and how she had found out about the fact that he was involved with another woman. They were at his apartment getting hot and heavy when his doorbell rang. At first, he pretended not to hear it, but when the visitor began to constantly push the button, Monique advised him to go and see who it was. Reluctantly, he got up and headed to the door, leaving her lying in his bed naked as the day she was born. Moments later, when she heard the sound of arguing coming from the front of the house, Monique jumped up. She wasn't sure what was going on, but she didn't want to be literally caught with her pants down. Monique was in the process of slipping her dress over her head when the bedroom door burst open.

"Who the fuck is this?" a female voice yelled, making her way inside the room towards Monique.

The lighter skinned woman looked at Monique in shock for a second, before there was fire in her eyes. Her beautiful face twisted into a horrible scowl when she looked down and noticed that the woman in her boyfriend's bedroom was naked from the waist down. She glanced back at him and from the look on his face, he knew he was caught. There was nothing more to say. Monique locked eyes with the woman, but before she had a chance to explain that she didn't know that he was involved, the female pounced on her. Together, they fell back onto the bed, with Monique stuck at the bottom. Over and over again, the female swung, connecting her hits all over Monique's face and head. All of this went while Monique laid on the bed feeling helpless. There was absolutely nothing that she could do because her arms had been stuck inside her dress, and the way that the woman was sitting on her prevented Monique from doing anything to change that. As she continued to get hit, Monique flopped around like a fish out of water trying to free herself, but it was no use.

A few moments passed before the chick was lifted up by her guy friend, which allowed Monique enough time to get her limbs into the holes of her dress. She jumped up, slid her arms into her sleeves, and thought about fighting back. When she looked in the corner of the room and saw the female still trying to get at her and her guy friend pleading for her to just leave, Monique changed her mind. Not wanting to cause anymore drama, Monique decided to just leave. She didn't bother to put on her underwear, since she didn't really know where they had been thrown anyway, and without so much as a word, she shamefully jetted toward the door with her purse thrown over her shoulder and her shoes clutched in her hand.

Monique felt stupid for allowing the unknown woman to beat on her the way that she did, especially in front of her guy friend. Her entire drive home, all she thought about was the fact that she'd wished she would have run over to the chick and got a few licks in for herself. The only reason why she didn't was because she wasn't sure what would happen. The woman was more than likely the girlfriend after all, and who knows what would have gone down if she decided to try her luck. Monique had only known the guy for a few weeks, and after finding out that he had someone else in his life, she realized that she didn't really know him as much as she thought she did. Monique was pissed and couldn't believe that she allowed things to go down the way they did. She had never been scary and would always fight, even though she wasn't the best at it.

Monique had always been one of those chicks that you literally had to beat the shit out of. She was the type that would be getting her ass whipped, but still talking mad junk, like she was winning the fight. This went on even when she was younger. Even back then, Monique was always in the middle of some shit. Whether it be he-say she-say, her fucking somebody's man, or just plain old gossiping; she was the one who always had a hand in bullshit. There had been plenty times that her mother had to drag her in the house after she had gotten beat down for running her mouth. Even that didn't stop Monique, who would still be talking shit out of the window of her bedroom, which would result in yet another fight the following day. Monique had a reputation for getting her ass kicked, but that didn't stop her from swinging on someone as if she was the best fighter in the neighborhood and it was because she had the heart of a lion.

"I don't know who the fuck—" *Slap* "you think you be talking to—" *Punch* "But you got the right mutha'fucker today, bitch!" Monique yelled as she pounded on her daughter. Since she couldn't take her anger out on the chick who had beat her ass earlier, she figured that her oldest would have to do.

"Ahhhh!" Dominique screeched when her mother grabbed a hand full of her hair and snatched her off of her bed. She was fully awake now. As soon as Dominique's knees landed on the carpeted floor, they immediately began to sting from the carpet burn. Although it hurt like hell, it was the least of Dominique's worries because her mother continued to hit her over and over again. The assault that she was receiving couldn't have been all because she didn't clean up the kitchen after her younger brother and sisters because she was sure that it wasn't that bad. No, this ass whooping was about something else. What that was, she had no idea. Her mother was fighting her as if she were a stranger on the street and this confused Dominique.

It wasn't the first time that Monique had put her hands on her daughter. In fact, she hit Dominique a lot. She'd smack her for not doing the dishes, or helping one of the kids with their homework. She only remembered one other instance when her mother had beat her this badly, and it had been a few years ago. Dominique felt helpless because what she really wanted to do was get up from the floor and blast her mother right in her fucking face. She wanted to show Monique how much it hurt to be hit on. Dominique knew that she couldn't do that because not only was it unacceptable to hit one of your parents, but she also knew how her mother was. Monique would call the police on her without a second thought and have her taken to juvenile. Even though that would be a better situation than practically being your mother's in-house slave, Dominique didn't want to leave her brothers and sisters behind. Because of this, Dominique continued to take the beating her mother was giving her, even though she felt herself on the brink of losing her patience.

In order to cushion the blows that Monique was throwing, Dominique attempted to curl up into a ball. It proved to be harder than she expected because the way that her mother was jerking her head from side to side made it almost impossible. Dominique screamed and bit down on her bottom lip to keep herself from lashing out. Monique was taking the shit too far, and Dominique knew that it was only a matter of time before she would no longer be responsible for her actions. Dominique understood that she had messed up by not cleaning the kitchen thoroughly like her mother had asked, but being Monique's punching bag was quickly getting old. At the point of no return,

Dominique balled up her fist. Her mother didn't know it, but she was about to be wearing a black eye her damn self.

"Stop mommy!" Tiffany screamed.

She had heard and saw enough. Tossing her covers off of her body, she jumped out of the bed. Quickly, she made her way over to her mother and tried her hardest to pry her hands off of her sister's hair. Monique swatted at her younger daughter with her free hand, while still holding a tight grip onto Dominique with the other. Tiffany didn't stop though, and continued to pull at her mother's fingers. This angered Monique because in her mind, Tiffany was choosing Dominique over her.

That was always the case in their household. Even her ex-husband, Jessie, loved their oldest daughter more than he loved his own wife. Monique thought back about how the bastard always put Dominique on a pedestal like she was a fucking princess, while he beat her ass every chance he got, sometimes for absolutely nothing. Monique was glad that his ass was gone because now she could do what the fuck she wanted, and everyone, including hardheaded ass Dominique, had no choice but to respect it or get they asses beat.

"Get the fuck off me!" Monique screamed. She let go of Dominique's hair and shoved Tiffany with both hands with all her might. The fourteen-year-old flew across the room and landed on her butt directly in front of her bed.

Monique's chest heaved up and down as she stared at her younger daughter for a moment, daring her to say or do anything that would grant her an ass whopping as well. Monique briefly contemplated on if she should just beat Tiffany's ass, just for the fact that she meddled in business that didn't concern her, but decided to just leave her alone. At that moment, Dominique was her issue, and she was the one who Monique wanted to punish. Plus, Tiffany was never really a problem. She just did dumb shit sometimes, and it always had something to do with Dominique. Tiffany always made good grades and did everything that Monique told her to do with no problems. She just happened to love her sister. Monique couldn't figure out why everyone adored Dominique so much and couldn't wait until the day that people realized that Dominique didn't care about anyone but her damn self. She was a selfish bitch who, for some reason, captured the hearts of others. Monique knew that eventually Tiffany was going to get a firsthand lesson on how self-centered her sister was, and once that happened, she would stand there with the 'I told you so' face.

"Yo' dumb ass gone get enough of taking up for this bitch!" Monique yelled, pointing down at Dominique, who was still sitting on the floor. "She doesn't give a fuck about you for real. Do you think she would have helped you if you were getting your ass beat?" Tiffany didn't respond right away. She was too afraid of what her mother would do if she said the wrong thing. "I asked you a muthafucking question, so I expect an answer. Do you think this bitch would help you if you were on the floor getting yo' ass beat?"

"Yea...yeah, I know that she would help me," Tiffany stammered. She knew, without a doubt, that if the shoe was on the other foot, Dominique would have helped her with no hesitation.

"I swear you are a fucking idiot; you know that?" Monique rolled her eyes and shook her head. "You can think what the fuck you want, but I tell you one goddamn thing." She paused, before she took a few steps in Tiffany's direction and pointed her finger in her face. "If you ever in yo' mutha'fucking life call yo'self getting in the middle of some shit that is going down between me and *anybody,* I will beat you down so fucking bad that I will have to keep you out of school for a week. Do you fucking hear me?"

"Yes," Tiffany muttered.

"Yes, what?"

"Yes ma'am."

"Good." Monique smirked. She was pleased by the terrified look on her daughter's face. "And you," she said, turning back to Dominique, "get yo' monkey ass up and clean my goddamn kitchen right fucking now, before I punch you in your ugly ass face again!"

Chapter Two

With tears still rolling down her face, Dominique quickly wiped them away before she finally stood from the floor. She knew that if she continued to cry, her mother would get mad all over again and try to hit her. She didn't want that, so she sucked in her tears and headed toward the kitchen praying that none escaped from her eyelids and fell against her will. When Dominique saw the mess her siblings had made, she wanted to scream. She didn't understand how there was cereal everywhere when she'd fixed them all French fries and chicken nuggets for dinner. A few moments later, she came to the conclusion that they must have gotten back out of bed after she fell asleep and made the mess that she saw before her. Dominque wanted to kick herself for not making sure that they were sleep before she dozed off, but she was just so tired that she couldn't help it.

With her head hung low, she sighed and began the task of cleaning up after them. She walked over to the table and picked up the discarded cereal box. A quick glance at the clock on the stove let her know that it was almost four in the morning. She had a little less than two hours before she had to wake her brothers and sisters up for school and make them breakfast. Dominique knew that the mess that they had created would take her a minute to clean up, so going back to sleep was more than likely out of the question; not that she could go back after the beating she received anyway. The fact that she had just gone to bed a little after eleven didn't give her much time to sleep. Dominique knew that she would pay for her lack of rest later that day at school; she just hoped that it wouldn't be too bad.

The sound of her mother entering her bedroom made Dominique turn to look in that direction. When the door closed behind her and she heard the lock click, Dominique rolled her eyes. She couldn't stand her mother sometimes. No, that was a lie, she couldn't stand her mother all of the time. Monique was a pain in her ass, and Dominique couldn't wait until she was old enough to get the fuck out of her house. Once she left, she wasn't looking back, no matter what the case was. Monique could officially kiss her ass once she turned eighteen, and she didn't give a damn how she felt about it. The only way she would come back was to visit her brothers and sisters, and that's it. It was sad to say, but Dominique always prayed that when Monique left the house to meet up with the random guys she'd come across, that one day she wouldn't come back. That's just how much she disliked, no scratch that, that was just how much she hated her mother.

If Monique wasn't forcing Dominique to take care of all of her younger siblings, she had her doing something else. From cooking, to cleaning, to washing, and everything in between, one would think that Dominique was the mother and Monique was the child. Monique came and went when she pleased and did nothing but layup with different men, bark out orders, spend her disable children's social security checks, and boss Dominique around. It seemed like ever since her father went to jail four years prior, Monique had showed her ass. It wasn't like she was the best mother then, but at least she attempted to put up a front because her husband kept her in line. Now, she didn't give a damn. Dominique wished that her daddy was back home because Monique wouldn't get away with half the shit she was doing. Truthfully, it should be her locked away and not him because she was more deserving of prison.

"I already know you're going to tell your daddy that I beat that ass, but I don't give a fuck."

Dominique jumped when she heard her mother's voice. She had been so caught up in her own thoughts that she didn't hear Monique's door open, or her come back out of her room. She turned to face her mother, but dropped her eyes because she didn't want to give Monique a reason to hit her again. With the way she was feeling at that moment, she was liable to spazz out and that would lead to Monique being put on her ass.

"Yeah, you didn't think I knew you were telling him about everything that was going on in my fucking house, huh?" Monique asked, before taking a long pull of the cigarette that now dangled between her fingers. Dominque hated the smell of the cancer sticks, but she wouldn't dare tell her mother that. "He told me to stop treating you like my slave," she scoffed. "I'm wondering how I can treat you like a slave when you don't do shit around here. I pay all these fucking bills, while you walk around like you are a queen or some shit. You don't pay for shit in this house!" Monique screamed.

Bitch, you don't either. Social security pays for everything with those checks, Dominique thought to herself.

"Now I wonder why he would think that I treat you like a slave."

"I don't know—" Dominque started.

"Bitch, stop lying!" Monique roared, cutting her off. "He's already passed a message through his funky ass mammy. Franny is lucky I don't report both they asses because last time I checked, that bastard isn't supposed to have *any* contact with me, and sending messages through another person is still considered having contact." Monique exhaled, releasing a cloud of smoke from her mouth. "Now, run and tell that mutha'fucka exactly what I said because it ain't like he can do shit about it," she told Dominique, giving her a stare down.

Monique really wanted her daughter to say

something out of pocket, so that she could bust her in the face again. She despised Dominique with a passion and most of the time she wished that she was never born. It was because of the pregnancy with her that Monique ended up with Jessie's fucked up in the head ass in the first place. Had she not had gotten pregnant with Dominique, she wouldn't have had to settle and been stuck with all those damn kids. Of course, that wasn't Dominique's fault, but according to Monique's logic, it was.

"It's funny how you can tell yo' daddy all the shit that I do around this mutha'fucka, but I ain't told him nothing about how sneaky and trifling yo' ass is, now did ya?" Monique questioned. When she saw Dominique drop her eyes, she knew that she had struck a nerve. She smacked her lips before she went ,on, "Don't get all shy now. How about the next time you talk to your daddy, you let him know how much of a hoe is daughter has become since he's been gone? Tell him all about what I caught you doing in my bedroom last year, and see what he has to say about that." With no more words spoken, Monique turned around and headed back into her room once again, this time, slamming the door behind her.

"What in the world is she rambling about now?" Tiffany murmured while walking into the kitchen.

"I don't know." Dominique shrugged.

"She kills me acting all tough now, knowing she wouldn't say any of that shit if daddy were out."

"Yeah, you're right," Dominique agreed, watching her mother's door to make sure that she hadn't reemerged again, "and you better stop cursing before she hears you," she chastised her sister. "Let me get this kitchen cleaned before it's time to wake everybody up for school. You can go back to bed, I got it."

"No, I'm going to help you," Tiffany told her, grabbing the broom. "I feel bad about you getting in trouble. I knew I should have just woken you up, but you looked so tired."

"Tired wasn't even the word. I was exhausted," Dominique explained, walking over to the kitchen sink. "Even then, it ain't your fault. It's your mothers." She glanced towards the door again. "If she'd get off her ass and help around here, I wouldn't have to do everything."

"Don't try to put her on me. That's yo' momma,

you're the oldest," Tiffany rebutted. "Plus, I don't even like the heffa." Dominique busted out laughing, but quickly brought her hand up to cover her mouth when she realized just how loud she was.

"Y'all better shut the fuck up in there before you wake up those kids!" Monique yelled from her room.

"I can't stand that bitch," Tiffany grunted.

"Me either."

"I should go in there and smother her ass with a pillow while she sleeps."

"You are so crazy." Dominique giggled quietly. She wished it were that easy to rid their mother out of their lives, but she knew better. Monique was like the devil and wasn't going anywhere with her evil ass.

After the sisters finished laughing at their mother's expense, both girls began the task of cleaning the kitchen. Dominique cleared off the table and washed the dishes, while Tiffany straightened up, swept, and mopped the floor. While they cleaned, they quietly talked about their plans for the weekend. Dominique hoped that she would be able to attend the neighborhood party with her boyfriend Kaleb, her other sister NiChia, and her best friend, Shanice. Tiffany, on the other hand, wanted to go skating with a few of her classmates. Both girls knew that with how funny acting Monique was, them being able to go out anywhere was a long shot, but they prayed that this would be a time where she wouldn't be so bad. It was easier said than done because Monique never let them go anywhere but to their grandmother's house, and even then, it wasn't often.

As they continued to talk, Dominique laughed and joked as if she were in good spirits, but deep down, she was still thinking about what her mother had said. Monique may not have known it, but that night haunted her daughter daily, even though she tried her best to forget about it. Dominique felt bad for lying to Tiffany when she told her that she had no clue what Monique was referring to. She knew exactly what her mother was talking about and was glad that her sister took her word for it and didn't push the issue. Dominique would have hated to try to explain to Tiffany all the things that had actually gone down. Those details were too much for a fourteen-year-old to know, and Dominique wanted her sister to not only keep her innocence as long as possible, but to not look at her differently.

The incident that Monique had brought up was yet another reason why Dominique hated her mother so much. While Monique thought that it was funny to throw it up in her face, Dominique knew deep down that she was actually upset about it; she just tried her best to hide it. The truth of the matter was it wasn't Dominique's fault and she was almost certain that her mother already knew that. Back when Dominique tried to explain everything to her, she was quickly shut down with a fist to the face. Monique beat her so bad that day that there are still marks across her back and thighs. After the ass whipping she received, Dominique never brought it up again; she knew better than to do so because Monique made it clear that she didn't want to hear anything that she had to say.

By the time the girls were through cleaning up the entire kitchen, it was almost time to wake up all of the children. Dominique went into the fridge and started breakfast, while Tiffany pulled out the ironing board and began to get everyone's outfits ready for the day. When they were done, together they went around the house and woke all of the kids up before helping them with their hygiene. As they all ate breakfast, Dominique smiled over at Tiffany. She was happy that her little sister had decided to stay up with her because she definitely helped her a lot. As always, she was grateful for Tiffany and felt bad that she had gotten in trouble behind her earlier. Dominique knew that Monique hated that they were so close. With them being only two years apart, Dominique and Tiffany were the closest of all of their eight siblings. Not only did they share a room, but they shared a bond that Monique was extremely jealous of. Tiffany wasn't just a little sister to Dominique; she was more like one of her best friends. Dominique loved her sister dearly and hated when Monique tried to put her against her. She hoped that it would never work because she couldn't imagine what she would do without Tiffany in her life.

After the children were fed and all of them were dressed, Dominique and Tiffany prepared for their long exhausting day of school, while Monique slept peacefully with her door locked, as if she didn't have a care in the world.

Chapter Three

"You know I love you right?" Kaleb asked, as he leaned down and planted a soft kiss on Dominique's lips.

"I know you do. I love you too." She smiled.

Her eyes closed involuntarily when he slipped his tongue deep into her mouth. She accepted his invitation with some tongue of her own before she threw her arms around his shoulders. Together, they laid on their sides in Kaleb's bed, each lost in their own worlds. Kaleb ran his hands slowly down from her back until he gripped her hips and pulled her lower body closer to his. A moan escaped his lips when Dominique didn't stop him from rolling her over. With her now on her back, Kaleb lifted up and climbed on top of her, with Dominique opening her legs slightly to receive him.

"Kaleb," she whined, when he tried to slip his hands into her pants.

"Damn Nikki, what?" Kaleb groaned, propping himself up with his arms.

"You already know what, so stop playing," she snapped.

After roughly pushing him off of her, she sat up and scooted towards the edge of the bed. Dominique folded her arms across her chest tightly. She wanted to let him know that she now had an attitude. Disappointed, Kaleb let out a forced breath, climbed out of the bed, and walked over by the window. He stared outside for a moment, at nothing in particular, before he dropped his eyes to the floor. It was very rare that they had time to be alone because there was always someone around. Dominique's house was not only filled with children all day, but her mother wouldn't even allow him to darken her door, so being alone with each other there was a definite no-no.

When it came to his house, his mother, Kendra, was always home taking care of Kendall, who was his eleven year old brother. Kendall suffered from *Duchenne Muscular Dystrophy*, which was a genetic disease that caused rapid muscular deterioration. Because of his illness, Kendra was forced to quit her job at the hospital as a RN and work from home doing case studies instead. That day, she happened to be taking Kendall to one of his many doctor's appointments and would be gone for the rest of the morning. When his mom told Kaleb about her plans, his first thought was Dominique. He figured that since they were never alone, they could cut school and finally do some of the things that he had been daydreaming about. Dominique accepted his offer to come over, but her reasons were different.

She was still kind of sleepy from the night before and didn't really want to be in school in the first place. It wasn't like she could stay home because with Monique there, she would only have her working. Dominique thought that by going over to Kaleb's, they would probably talk, watch a movie, or maybe even go to sleep. Not once did she think that he was only inviting her over because he thought that they were going to have sex. She thought that he just wanted to spend time with her.

Kaleb brought his eyes up to hers and asked, "What's the problem now?"

"There's no problem," she told him simply.

"Then why did you stop me?"

Dominique looked at him sideways before she replied, "Because you know damn well that I didn't come over here to fuck you. You already know how I feel about that."

"Come on Nikki, how long are you going to make me wait?" he inquired. "I love you and you love me, so I don't really see why this is such a big issue."

"I'm not about to keep having this same damn conversation with you, Kaleb. When we first got together, I told yo' ass how I felt about having sex and you said that you were cool with it. Now, you *all of a sudden* have a problem. Make up your damn mind. One second, you understand and the next, you don't. Which one is it because I'm tired of the back and forth shit?" Dominique sassed. Her right leg began to rock back and forth, which was a sign that she was getting upset.

"Yeah, I said I was cool with it back then because I was. That was two years ago, Nikki. I honestly had no clue that you were going to be still acting like this after all this time. I've been asking about this shit for the last few months, and you keep giving me the exactly same answer."

"So, shouldn't that tell you something?" she asked with her fact twisted up.

Dominique was already tired, so arguing with her boyfriend was not something she wanted to do, especially about the same subject that they had gone over time and time again. They had already had words with one another in the hallway before they left school. Kaleb flipped when he saw that Dominique had a black eye, even though she tried her best to cover it with concealer. He was livid. Dominique explained that it was nothing, but Kaleb threatened to send someone over to her house to show Monique what it felt like to be punched in the eye. Dominique begged him not too, not because she cared about her mother getting hurt, but because she didn't want him to get in trouble if it came out that he was the one behind it. After talking some sense into him about that and calming him down, they still ended up arguing hours later.

Dominique was getting fed up of repeating herself. She had told Kaleb from the very beginning that she didn't plan on having sex until she was married, and at first, he agreed to be celibate with her. He claimed that he understood her reasoning and that he was glad to have a 'good girl', but now, he was singing another tune. Now it seemed like every time she turned around, he was bringing it up and she was sick of it.

"Whatever man," Kaleb sighed, "just tell me when and I'll stop asking you about it."

"When what?" Dominique asked with wide eyes.

"When we are going to finally make it happen? We've been together long enough for you to know that I'm not just gone hit it and quit it. You'll let me kiss all on you or suck ya titties, but nothing past that." He stopped and looked at her. "It's like when I start working my way below the waist, you freeze up. Why let me do all that if you ain't gone do nothing but stop me? If you don't want me to go there, you shouldn't get me started in the first place. It's like you teasing me and shit."

"Teasing you? If I'm not mistaken, you were the one who kissed me," Dominique responded, surprised by how far he was taking it.

"Yeah, but you ain't stop me. You kissed me right back."

"Okay, and? I did that because I want to kiss my

boyfriend. I like to be close to you sometimes. Is there something wrong with that?"

"Hell yeah, there's something wrong with that!" Kaleb retorted. "You get me all riled up, only to shut me down. I swear you be playing games and shit," he told her, pacing back and forth across the floor.

"Shut the hell up Kaleb because right now, you are doing the most. Ain't nobody playing no games with you."

"You could've fooled the hell outta me." He took a few steps closer to her before he continued. "Look Nikki, I'm sorry, but I'm just getting irritated with the situation," he told her honestly. "I know we're young, but I have needs."

"Needs my ass Kaleb! Your only seventeen, what kind of needs could you possibly have?" she grunted, while rolling her eyes up in her head. He was really starting to piss her off. "You act like you did the shit before. You're a virgin your damn self, so stop trying to act like you've been fucking for years!"

"See, now you trying to play me, when you know that ain't got shit to do with it! I ain't gotta have done it to want to do it," he explained. "You got me walking around looking dumb as hell. Niggas in school bragging about all the pussy they getting, while I'm sitting there quiet as hell. Shit, everybody is doing it but us."

"First of all, I ain't making you look like shit. If you're looking dumb, stupid, or whatever, then that's all on you, playa, so don't try to put that shit on me," she told him, rolling her neck. "Second, I don't give a damn about everybody else, Kaleb! I don't do what everybody else is doing. I'm my own fucking person, and you knew from jump that I wasn't like all these other lil' bitches who be quick to give up the ass. Those are the hoes that the niggas are bragging about. So, if that's what you want, then I'm sorry, but you have the wrong girl. I thought you understood that already."

"I know you are your own person, and that's why I love you," Kaleb professed, softening his tone. "I just want to know how long you expect me to wait, Nikki. I love you and you love me. I've already told you that we're getting married as soon as we graduate, so why do we have to continue to wait?"

"Because, we're *not* married yet, Kaleb! Not only that, but anything can happen between now and graduation. Look how you're acting right now, like a little ass fucking kid!"

"That's bullshit and you know it!" Kaleb yelled. "I have never given you any reason to believe that I would leave you, so you reaching like hell for saying some shit like that to me. Do you know how many bitches be throwing me the pussy?" he asked, but as soon as the question left his lips, he instantly regretted it.

The look on Dominique's face let him know that he had fucked up royally. It was a mixture of hurt, embarrassment, and anger, all in one. Kaleb immediately wished that he could rewind time and take back the words that just spilled out of his mouth like vomit, but he knew he couldn't. It was too late, and the damage had already been done. Not knowing what else to do, he braced himself for the storm ahead.

"Humph," Dominique snorted. She stood up, snatched her purse off of his bed, and walked directly up to him. With her finger just inches from his face, she calmly told him, "Well, I guess you should find all those bitches that are throwing you pussy and go fuck with them then because I'm done with yo' simple stupid ass."

"Wait Nikki, I didn't mean it like that," Kaleb said desperately as he jumped in front of her, as she headed to his door. He put his arm out, blocking her way. "Can you just sit back down and talk to me?" he asked with pleading eyes. "You know that shit didn't come out right. You know I would never say nothing like that to you."

With her eyes watering, Dominique looked at her boyfriend and said barely above a whisper, "Fuck you, Kaleb. Get the hell out of my way," before she shoved him with all her might.

She rushed over to his bedroom door and slung it open so hard, it slammed into the wall behind it. As she headed towards the front of the house, she could hear Kaleb walking behind her as she neared the exit. Pulling the front door open, Dominique stomped down the porch steps. She used the back of her hand to wipe away the tears that were slowly rolling down her cheeks. Her feelings were hurt, and she was still shocked at the fact that Kaleb had acted that way towards her. In the two years that they've been together as a couple, he had been nothing but a gentleman to her. *Is he really getting fed up with waiting for me to give up the goods?* She asked to herself. By the time she got to the end of his street, she turned and looked back at his house. The fact that he hadn't chased behind her made Dominique feel even worse.

Maybe he is tired.

She thought about going back, but quickly decided against it. There was no way in hell that she was going to kiss his ass. If Kaleb wanted to have an attitude about her not wanting to fuck him, that was on him. He could go to hell for all she cared. Dominique was angry and wished that she would have just stayed her ass at school. As she made her way to the bus stop a few streets over, she had time to calm down and actually think about everything. Dominique knew deep in her gut that Kaleb didn't mean for the words to come out like they had. Of course, she knew that there were girls who threw themselves at him. He was one of the cutest boys in school, so she would be a fool not to believe that. Kaleb had just let his anger get the best of him, just like she had. Dominique knew that she didn't mean it when she told him that she was done with him. The truth was that they had both said some things that neither of them meant. Dominique figured they both needed time to cool down and when the air was clear, they would talk.

Now, at the bus stop, Dominique took a seat on the bench. As she watched the many cars whizz by, she thought about her situation. She didn't have a normal life like other sixteen year olds. She couldn't stay out late, hang out with her friends, or have slumber parties like the other girls in school. In fact, she could barely come outside at all because her mother wouldn't allow her to do anything other than watch after the kids. This put a strain on her relationship with Kaleb; a relationship that Dominique was surprised had lasted that long. If she would have been a guy, she knew for sure that she wouldn't even think to date the girl who could never do anything but stay in the house. Dominique could barely talk on the phone, which is why her and Kaleb's relationship was strictly something that happened at school.

Taking all of those things into consideration, Dominique began to grasp the fact that maybe Kaleb actually had a right to be upset. He had been patient with her and up until that day, he had done a damn good job of being a great boyfriend. The two of them loved one another and had plans to marry once they finished school. After, she would go to college, while he got a job until he could purchase his first property, which he would flip and start all over again. They would have two children and raise them in a loving home. Kaleb and Dominique had their entire lives planned out and although she knew that it wouldn't be perfect like they predicted, Dominique was willing to stick it out with him.

Maybe I should just go ahead and do it, she rationalized with herself.

Right away, Dominique wished that it was as easy as it seemed like it should have been. She wished that it was just simply her lying down and allowing him to make love to her. It wasn't though, and she didn't know how exactly to explain that to Kaleb because she knew that he wouldn't understand. Things were different now and just the thought of telling him what she was forced to hide was enough to make her sick to her stomach. Dominique knew that, eventually, she would have to open up and share her secret because if Kaleb were to hear it from someone else, mainly her mother, he wouldn't believe anything she said afterwards and would swear that she was in fact just playing games.

By the time the bus pulled up, Dominique had come

to a conclusion. She was going to tell Kaleb everything after the party the following night. She just hoped that he wouldn't look at her differently after she told him that she was no longer a virgin, like he believed her to be.

Chapter Four

"**K**eep your head up Pumpkin, and don't let your dumb ass mother drive you too crazy," Jessie said to his daughter the following day. "You don't have long before you'll be going away for college and away from her evil ass for good," he told her seriously.

Dominique giggled, "I know daddy and I can't wait."

"I know you can't. Just stick it out and keep making your daddy proud. You hear me?"

"I most certainly will."

I love you baby girl," he told her, hating the fact that they had to get off the phone.

"I love you too daddy and I'll talk to you next week," Dominique replied, right before the operator disconnected the call.

They had just had a fifteen-minute conversation about everything under the sun in that short amount of time. Jessie had asked his daughter about school, his other children, and life in general, like he always did. Even with him being locked away, he still cared about all of his children's wellbeing and always wanted to make sure that they were okay, even though his ex-wife refused to let him speak to most of them. That is why when Dominique told him about how Monique was treating her, he lost it; even after he'd promised that he wouldn't. Jessie didn't play any games when it came to his children, especially his Pumpkin, and Monique knew that.

Dominique was not only Jessie's first born, but she also had a special place in his heart as well. One of the reasons was the fact that she was a splitting image of him. They looked exactly alike, with the same color skin tone and bright round eyes. His parents used to always joke that Dominique was the girl version of Jessie, and whenever they were all together, they would always pull out the photo album and put both of their baby pictures side by side to prove their point. Not only were they twins, but Dominque acted just like her father. Both were very kind-hearted, loving, and would give you the shirt off of their backs. The flip side of that was that they were both ticking time bombs. If pushed too far, they were both liable to cause damage to anyone in their way once they got angry. Dominique knew what her father was capable of from the many times that she sneakily looked on while he beat her mother, and that is why she really didn't want to tell him what was going on inside his old home.

Once she did, Jessie's blood boiled. He knew that the only reason that Monique was treating Dominique that way was because she knew that he could no longer do anything about it. Monique was not only a very spiteful person, but she had always been jealous of the way that he treated his daughter. She used to complain all of the time about how if it came down to it, he would choose Dominique over her. Jessie never actually argued with her about it because what she was saying was the truth. He did love his daughter more and hated that he had to leave her alone with her bitch of a mother. The choice was not his to make though and one event made sure of that. Once he was arrested and hauled off to jail, he began to question the decisions that he'd made many years prior.

Jessie McDonald had just begun his senior year of high school and it was then that he encountered Monique. Their union was not one of a storybook romance. In fact, it was quite the opposite. One day at one of the basketball games held at their school, they struck up a conversation. Monique had always thought that Jessie was cute and wanted to see what was up with the quiet guy that all the girls secretly liked. That evening, one thing led to another, and they ended up having sex in the back of Jessie's car. Since Monique was always known as an easy kind of girl, Jessie didn't bother to give her a second glance after it was all said and done. Because of the reputation she carried, he knew he was nothing special, considering that he'd heard rumors about all of the other guys that she'd been with. In Jessie's eyes, it was nothing more than one night of sex and he was fine with that.

That was, until Monique showed up at his door a few weeks later letting him know that she was pregnant and that he was the father. Right away, Jessie didn't believe her because he knew for a fact that he wasn't the only person that she had slept with, and he told her exactly that before telling her to get the hell away from his house. They began to argue back and forth, which caught the attention of his mother, Franny, who came to the door to see what was going on. Upon hearing what her son had gotten himself into, she told Monique that if the baby was Jessie's, that they would step up and help her to provide for the child. This was a shock to Monique, who only came over to Jessie's to see if she could get some abortion money. She didn't want to have a baby at all because she knew that it would alter her lifestyle. Unfortunately for her, neither of Jessie's parents believed in abortions. It didn't help that her mother refused to give her a dime and told her, 'You laid yo' ass down and got pregnant, now you deal with it'.

Eight months later, Dominique was born and as soon as everyone laid eyes on her, they all knew that there was no doubt that she was indeed Jessie's. Immediately, Jessie and his family stepped up and started to help provide for the beautiful baby girl who looked just like her father did when he was that age. They purchased everything that Dominique needed, from the crib to clothes and everything in between. In fact, Jessie's parents all but moved Dominique in. They had her over their house more than she was at home with her mother; which was okay with her because she didn't really want the child in the first place. If it were up to Monique, they could have taken Dominique forever and she wouldn't have cared one bit.

A few weeks later, they all learned what they pretty much already knew and that was that Jessie was, in fact, the father of Dominique. With the DNA results in hand, Jessie called Monique over and proposed to her right there in the living room of his parents' house. Jessie's offer to marry her had absolutely nothing to do with love because he didn't feel that way about Monique at all. He proposed because he knew that it was the right thing to do, since she was the mother of his child. Although his parents didn't think that it was a good idea, his mother especially, they stood behind their son and promised to help him out as much as they could. Taken back, Monique said yes to be Jessie's wife. Of course, she didn't love him either or the child that she had just given birth to. She agreed to get married only because she saw it as a way out. Not only did she desperately want to get away from her abusive, alcoholic mother, but she knew that Jessie came from a well off family and she wanted to capitalize on it.

A little over a month later, Jessie graduated and the following week, they were married in a small ceremony in his parents' backyard. As a wedding present, Jessie's father gave him the paperwork to the construction company that he owned. With him retiring soon, he wanted his son to take over the business, which was always the plan that he had. This made Jessie happy because not only did he want to make his parents proud, but he was looking forward to being able to provide for his small family. Monique, on the other hand, was ecstatic because she knew that she had finally caught a good one. Seeing that her husband was on his way to the big bucks, the eighteen-year-old Monique immediately dropped out of high school. Her actions didn't come as a shocker to anyone because she was only in the ninth grade to begin with. Other than being cute, dressing nice, and having a killer body, Monique didn't have anything else going for her. Now that she was married, she figured she could ride off of Jessie's coattail for as long as he allowed her to.

By the time Dominique was one, Jessie had saved

up enough money for a down payment to move them out of his parents' house and into their own. It was a four bedroom, two and a half brick townhouse that Monique absolutely loved. With Jessie giving her the okay, she busied herself decorating each of the rooms exactly the way she wanted. Once the home was completely furnished, Monique invited her mother and a few of her family members over. That was only a onetime thing because after a fight broke out between her mother and aunt, Jessie banned them all from coming back to their house. Monique didn't care either way because she had only invited her family over so that she could rub her new cushy lifestyle in their faces. After that was done, she didn't care if she'd ever saw either one of them again.

Things were going pretty good in the beginning. Jessie was running the construction company, and Monique had settled into being a stay at home mom. She tried her best to bond with her child, but her motherly instincts just never clicked. While Jessie was away at work, Monique pretty much allowed Dominique to do whatever it was that she wanted, while she sat around drinking and watching soap operas.

Monique struggled to keep her old self locked up, but it was extremely hard. She had never pictured herself as a mother, and even though she was in fact one, she didn't want to stay cooped up in the house all of the time with a daughter that she didn't even want. Being a homebody was slowly driving Monique insane, but she suppressed it as much as she could because she knew just how much she could lose if she didn't.

That tactic worked for a few years before the signs really began to show. Jessie knew what his wife was capable of, so he steered her on a clear path as much as he could. He was no fool though and knew that it was only a matter of time before Monique started to fall back into her old habits again. Right after Dominique turned two, Monique had Tiffany and it seemed like every other year after that, she was pregnant again. By the time they were both twenty-seven, Monique had given birth to a total of seven children. Soon after, Jessie's best friend, Nicole, died from complications from diabetes, leaving behind her nine-year-old daughter, NiChia. With the child having nowhere else to go, Jessie brought her home to raise with his children, bringing their total up to eight.

After NiChia came to live with them, Monique lost it. She was already overwhelmed with her own children. Having just given birth to their youngest child, Eva, Monique was trying her best to take care of the household, but it was tiresome. Not to mention, their one year old twins, Taylor and Skylar who had ADD. Just dealing with them day in and day out was a chore in itself. So, for Jessie to add one more to the bunch was just too much for Monique. She thought that Jessie was being inconsiderate because he wasn't the one who had to deal with the kids all day long. Not only that, but she didn't give two shits about Nicole dying because she never liked the bitch anyway.

Monique swore that Jessie and Nicole had fucked around while they were together, and NiChia was a product of their infidelity. She had no clue that, although NiChia was in fact Jessie's biological daughter, it wasn't because he had cheated on her. He and Nicole had had sex a few times right after he and Monique had hooked up. Nicole found out she was pregnant not long after, but didn't reveal the truth to Jessie. She led him to believe that she had gotten pregnant by a one-night stand. This tore Jessie up because he had always been secretly in love with her for as long as he could remember. He knew that he couldn't say much because he had slipped up himself and had a baby on the way. He didn't find out that NiChia was his until after she died.

Soon after, Jessie was contacted by a lawyer, who told him that Nicole had named him as a beneficiary of her life insurance policy. Jessie didn't think anything of it because Nicole had no family other than her aunt, and she couldn't stand her, so it made sense. Upon learning how much she'd left him, he was handed a letter handwritten by Nicole herself. In that letter, she revealed that NiChia was his daughter, and why she hadn't told him before then. Her reasoning was that Jessie was already expecting a baby with another female and that it had hurt her feelings. She went on to explain that she planned to tell him once NiChia was born, but once she found out that he and Monique were getting married, she decided to leave them be. She didn't want to bring drama in their fresh marriage, so she opted to keep it to herself. Nicole ended the letter, by letting Jessie know that she always loved him, before telling him to take care of their daughter. By the time

Jessie had finished reading, he was in tears. Had he known that Nicole felt the same way that he did, he would have never married Monique in the first place. Armed with the knowledge of having yet another child, Jessie kept that information to himself because he knew that his wife wouldn't understand. So he opted to pretend to adopt NiChia, and claim her as his child that way.

It didn't matter either way because right after their nine year anniversary, Monique tossed the married life to the side and went back to her old ways. She started to drop all of the kids off at Jessie's parents' house whenever she could, just to get away. They'd stay there for hours at a time until Jessie got off of work and brought them home. Drinking and smoking had become a way of life for Monique, and whenever there was a party in her old hood, she was in attendance. This lasted for a few months before Jessie had had enough. He kicked her out and changed the locks. This was music to Monique's ears, at first, because she was glad to finally be away from him and all of his nerve-wracking ass children. It didn't take long before she began to run out of money, and with no funds, all of her so-called "friends" turned their backs on her. Many of them wouldn't even let her sleep on their couch. It was then that Monique realized that she had seriously fucked up.

With nowhere else to go, Monique came crawling back to Jessie, with the promise that she would change. Even though he didn't believe her, Jessie allowed her to come back because not only was it hard for him to raise them and work at the same time, but he also knew that the kids needed their mother, no matter how shitty she was.

Monique's claim to 'do right' lasted for about a week, before she was at it again. This time, instead of putting her out of the house again, Jessie handled it a different way. When she called herself getting ready to walk out of the door, Jessie hauled off and smacked her down to the floor. She jumped up acting like she was bad, but after a few more licks, she surrendered and went back up to their room. It surprised Jessie when he noticed that afterwards Monique acted like she had sense for about a month. After that, Jessie figured that that must be the best way to keep her in line. Whenever Monique would act up, he would smack her around.

Jessie hated to put his hands on Monique, but if it meant that his children would have a mother at home with them, he was willing to do what he had to do.

This went on for the next three years. During that time, Monique had gotten better at hiding the things that she was doing. Since she couldn't get away with dropping the kids off at their grandparents anymore, she started to drink heavily at home. She would hide multiple bottles of liquor all around the house, and once Jessie was gone to work, she would spend her entire day getting drunk. She was able to get away without him noticing, all the way up until the birth of their last child, Jada.

When Jada was born, Jessie knew that something wasn't right with his daughter as soon as the nurse brought her over. Even though she was born eight weeks early, she was still much smaller than she should have been and truthfully, she didn't look normal at all. Jessie spoke up about it and was told by the doctor that he would run some test. When the results came back, Jessie found out that Jada was born with Fetal Alcohol Syndrome. To find that out was a shocker for him because he had no clue that his wife had been drinking during her pregnancy because he had never seen her. He knew that he worked a lot and wasn't home much, but to not find not one bottle of alcohol in their house made him realize that Monique had been keeping it a secret. Not able to keep calm, Jessie lost it right there inside the hospital room.

By the time security was able to pull him off of Monique, she was nothing but a bloody pulp lying on the floor. While the nurses tended to her, Jessie was arrested and carted off to jail. While Monique was only ordered to attend Alcoholic Anonymous classed, Jessie ended up being sentenced to ten years in prison. Once Monique found out that Jessie wasn't coming home, she served him with divorce papers. She was glad to be done with him and immediately went on to live her life, while he began to count down the days until he was a free man again.

"So, do you think she's going to let you go to the party?" NiChia asked, once Dominque was off the phone.

She hoped that Monique would allow Dominique to go because she was looking forward to spending time with her sister. She hadn't really had a chance to kick it with her because Monique tried her best to keep them apart. Once she found out that NiChia was actually Jessie's daughter, she treated her like the plague, and she was no longer welcome in her house. It happed right after Jessie was sentenced. Monique was getting rid of all of his stuff, when she stumbled upon the letter that Nicole had written years prior. Her saw nothing but red as she read line after line on the sheet of paper. Even though it was written that they hadn't had sex since they'd been together, Monique believed otherwise and thought that Jessie had a lot of nerve. He had been creeping with that bitch for years, yet he wanted to beat her ass for wanting to party, and taking a few drinks. In Monique's mind, Jessie was just as bad as she was. Immediately after finding the letter, she kicked NiChia out of her house and told her to never come back again.

"I hope so because I ain't trying to be stuck in the house babysitting all weekend," Dominique replied, rolling her eyes.

"I know that's right," NiChia agreed. "Yo' momma be acting like you laid down and had those kids. Ain't no way in hell you should have to take care of them while she runs the damn streets. I can't stand that woman," she told her, thinking about how terrible Monique used to treat her.

They were sitting on the couch at their grandmother's. Since Monique banned everything Jessie at their house, the only way that Dominique could speak to her father was when she was visiting Franny, which wasn't often at all. Now a widow, Franny always made sure that her phone bill was paid, so that her only child could communicate with the outside world. Her son was all she had left, after her husband, James, died of a stroke the year before Jessie went to prison. That was until Monique sent NiChia off to live with her. Even though Franny was much older now, she didn't bat an eye when she opened the door and saw NiChia standing there in the rain soaking wet with tears running down her face. Monique didn't even care that she had put a twelve year in a cab by herself in the middle of the night with nothing but a small book bag filled with her belongings and Franny's address. From that day forward, NiChia became Franny's responsibility, and she welcomed her with open arms. To Franny, it was just like old times when Nicole used to come over and stay day in and day out. Truth be told, she always wished that Jessie would have married Nicole instead of Monique; who in her opinion was a ghettofied hood rat.

"Nikki, are you ready?" Franny asked with her car keys in her hand.

"Yeah, I'm ready grandma," Dominique sighed.

She realized that she had to go home, but she didn't feel like it at all. From the conversation she had with her mother earlier that day, she already knew that Monique was in a bad mood and more than likely wasn't going to allow her go to the party. Dominique hoped that by bringing Franny along with her, her mother would take it easy and let her go. Since she hadn't seen or heard from Kaleb since the day before, she missed him dearly. While she wasn't looking forward to the conversation they needed to have, she just wanted to get it over with.

"Peanut, are you going or are you staying here?" Franny asked, calling NiChia by her nickname.

"I'll stay here, grandma!" she yelled back. "Call me and let me know what she says Nikki."

"Will do," Dominique promised, before they walked out of the door to make the thirty minute drive back to

Atlanta.

Chapter Five

"**D**idn't I mutha'fucking say no?" Monique hollered from her bedroom door. "I'm going out tonight, and you gotta watch the kids."

"But Ma, I'm always watching the kids," Dominique pouted. She felt brave knowing that her grandmother was there, and figured that Monique wouldn't touch her.

"Girl, you better get the fuck out my face before I beatcho' ass!" Monique warned. "You think because your grandmother is here, I won't knock yo' ass out? You better act like you know."

"Calm down Monique," Franny intervened. "How about I take the kids with me to my house while you go out? That way, Nikki can go to the party and have some fun for once."

Monique walked completely out of her room and into the kitchen. She looked at the older woman with a smirk on her face. She found it amusing how Franny was so quick to come to Dominique's rescue. Her lips quickly turned up into a scowl. Monique continued to stare at the pair as she thought about all of the times that she had asked Franny to watch the kids and had been turned down. Now that Little Miss Dominique wanted to go somewhere, Franny was offering to keep them all. Seeing the hopeful look on her daughter's face made Monique feel warm and tingly inside because she knew that she was about to wipe that stupid grin right off. There was no way in hell that she was going to allow Dominique to go anywhere, and it wasn't because she had some place to be. Truthfully, Monique had nowhere to go, but she would leave the house and drive around for hours before she allowed Dominique to have even a little bit of fun.

"I don't know why you looking happy and shit because I said no!" Monique yelled. "Now, get the fuck out of my face."

"Why do you always have to be such a bitch?" Franny asked, shocking Dominique, who had never heard her grandmother curse.

"Excuse me?" Monique asked, taken back. She chuckled when she realized that Franny was trying to jump bad. Taking a few steps in her ex-mother-in-law's direction, she asked, "What the fuck did you just say to me?"

"I said, why do you always have to be such a bitch?" Franny repeated, with no fear whatsoever. "You walk around here treating your kids like shit, just because you can. Do you ever stop and think about what you are doing to them...especially Dominique. You act like she's your personal assistant in this damn house! She's sixteen years old, and you got her taking care of *your kids,* cooking, cleaning, and everything else that you don't wanna do around this mutha'fucka! The damn girl never even gets a chance to do shit and that's all because of you." Franny twisted her neck and placed her hand on her hips.

"You need to get yo' old ass the fuck up out of my house right now, before I really tell you about yourself. You don't know what the fuck goes on in my household," Monique spoke. She glanced over at Dominique, who quickly dropped her eyes.

"I know enough. I know that you don't do shit but sit on your ass, cash these kids' social security checks, and give out orders like you the fucking queen of England or something." Franny was so upset; her usual caramel complexion was turning red. "There are some women who shouldn't have kids and you, my dear, are one of them. I knew I should have backed my son up when he told you to get the fuck off of our porch all those years ago. You were a piece of ghetto trash then, and you are a piece of ghetto trash now. We should've left you where Jessie found you, and that was in the gutter.

Monique moved at the speed of light and was in Franny's face before she knew it.

"Listen bitch," she said through clenched teeth, "you better watch how you speak to me in *my house* because I'm not above kicking yo' ass," Monique warned. "I suggest you take yo' wrinkly ass on home before you take me there. Yo' old ass limped up in here, but if you keep fucking with me, you gone end up crawling out. Don't believe me if you want to."

"You don't scare me bitc—" Before Franny had to chance to finish her sentence, Monique popped her in the mouth with a closed fist.

The two women began to tussle in the kitchen. Although Franny was more than twenty years older than Monique, she gave her a run for her money; that was until she tripped over one of the legs of the kitchen chair. At first, Dominique stood there stuck. She couldn't believe that her mother and grandmother were actually fighting. The sound of Tiffany screaming jolted Dominique out of her surprised state. She rushed over to where they were fighting and grabbed her mother by the back of her shirt, trying to get her off of Franny, who was now lying on the floor. When Monique felt her daughter tugging at her, she turned around slightly and swung on Dominique, hitting her square in the eye.

That was all it took. Dominique let go of her mother's shirt and grabbed chunks of her hair with both hands. She dragged her off of her grandmother backwards, and slung her into the adjacent wall. Monique recovered quickly and started to swing on Dominique rapidly, throwing punch after punch. Normally, this would be the time that Dominique would curl up in an attempt to protect her face, but today wasn't one of those days. Instead, Dominique hauled off and punched her mother so hard Monique immediately fell to the floor. Seeing her mother in such a vulnerable state triggered something inside her. Maybe it was all of the other times that she had been in that same position, while her mother beat on her time and again. Whatever the reason was, Dominique took advantage of the situation.

She leaned down and grabbed a chunk of her mother's hair again, this time with her left hand, and started to viciously punch her with the right. Monique screamed and tried to fight back, but it was no use, so she tried to curl up and protect her face. Ironically, it was the same thing that had gone down just days before. This time, Dominique was the one who was getting in the licks, and Monique was on the receiving end. While Dominique continued to hit her mother, she thought about all of the things that Monique had done to her. She was tired of her mother putting her hands on people and she was going to teach her a lesson. With each punch she delivered, she looked at it as pay back.

"Bitch, I'm gone show you!" Dominique yelled.

It was one thing for Monique to hit her, but to put her hands on her grandmother was a whole different thing. Monique was going to see how it felt to be hit and abused, and at that point, Dominique didn't care what the consequence was. She continued to punch her mother over and over again.

"That's enough, Dominique!" Hearing her grandmother's voice didn't even stop Dominique because at that moment, she was too far gone. "Stop it baby, please stop!" Franny yelled, placing her hand on Dominique's shoulder. "Help me Tiffany!"

With Tiffany joining in, they were able to successfully pry Dominique off of her mother, who was now wearing a bloody nose and busted lip. Monique jumped up ready to fight again. She rushed over towards where Franny and Tiffany were holding Dominique back with her fist balled up.

"Bitch, I should kill you!" she screamed, while taking a swing over Franny's head.

"No!" Franny yelled with her arm out, putting space between her and Dominique. "Leave her the fuck alone before I call the police. I don't think they'd want to hear anything you have to say after I tell them that you've assaulted me."

Those words halted Monique right in her tracks.

She was still ready to fuck Dominique up, but knew that if Franny called the police, no matter what she said about her daughter, she was going to go to jail. That was something that she didn't want, so she took a few steps back. She continued to look at Dominique with fire in her eyes, silently letting her know that the shit between the two of them was far from over.

"I'm taking her with me," Franny spoke.

She grabbed Dominique's arm and began to back up out of the kitchen. Before they made it through the door, her face contorted into a painful expression as she clutched her chest. Seconds later, she fell to the floor.

"Ahhh, my chest," Franny moaned.

Dominique hurried and bent down by her grandmother's side, while Tiffany stood in the corner crying hysterically. Monique, on the other hand, stared down at her ex-mother-in-law with fear in her eyes. She knew that more than likely their fight was the reason why Franny was on the floor struggling to breath. Monique was terrified. It wasn't Franny that she worried about because she could have died right there for all she cared. No, Monique was scared that she would be to blame for it. Franny's chest heaved up and down as she fought to catch her breath. She looked up at her granddaughter helplessly because she was truly scared that this was the end.

"Call 911!" Dominique screamed as tears spilled from her eyes. "Grandma, it's going to be okay." She cried, while saying a silent prayer.

Four days later, Dominique sat in a chair in her grandmother's hospital room. Franny had suffered a heart attack right there in her house and it was all because of her mother, and the fact that she could never learn to keep her hands to herself. Once the ambulance got there, they asked questions about what had happened leading up to her heart attack. Franny wouldn't disclose the fact that it was Monique who had put everything in motion. She simply said that she was there to pick up her granddaughter and fell as they made their way to the door. This pleased Monique, who had been worried sick from the time that 911 had been called, all the way up until the time they had arrived. She didn't want to go to jail, so Franny's lie was music to her ears.

Once at the hospital, Dominique asked her grandmother why she didn't tell on her mother, and Franny told her that she didn't because she didn't want the kids to be without their mother. She also reminded Dominique that she too could have gotten in trouble behind everything also because she had assaulted her mother as well. Dominique didn't care if she got in trouble; all she wanted was for Monique to pay for what she did. Dominique knew that what her mother had done was much worse, and at the end of the day, she could have easily say that she was protecting her grandmother, which wasn't a lie

The doctors had decided to keep Franny for one last day to finishing running test and make sure that she was officially in the clear to go home. He also told her that once she was released, she would have to start eating better and stop stressing so much over things. Eating better wasn't an issue for Franny because she had already started a path to healthy living a few weeks prior, but no stress was another issue. As a mother of a son in prison, she worried about Jessie day in and day out. Although she knew that he could take care of himself, the fear of the unknown scared her. He was incarcerated in a place filled with killers, so it was only right that she worried about him. He was her baby, after all.

"How is Franny doing now?" Shanice, Nikki's best friend, asked over the phone.

"She's doing a lot better. They just took her downstairs to run a few more tests, before they let her go home tomorrow," Dominique explained.

"Girl, I still can't believe yo' crazy ass momma fought yo' granny," Shanice exclaimed. "What's even more shocking is the fact that you jumped in and fought yo' momma! Now that's crazy."

"I know right? It felt good to jab her ass a few times." Dominique giggled.

"I swear I thought you were lying that day when you called me from the hospital and told me what had happened. I would have *never* believed no shit like that."

"Me either, but you should have seen how she was kicking and screaming on the floor while I was tagging her ass."

"Girl, I wish I was a fly on the wall."

"Her ass thought she could really handle me after all those times I let her hit me. I guess I showed her. You know I don't play about my grandma."

"I know you don't," Shanice agreed.

"Anyways, enough about that heffa. Tell me about the party. Did I miss anything?"

"It was okay, and yeah, you missed a lot."

"Damn, now I really wish I would have been able to go," Dominique said sadly. "Did you get a chance to tell Kaleb what I said?"

"Yeah, I did, but listen because I have something I have to tell you."

"Ummm, okay. What is it?" Dominique asked, worried by how her best friend's tone changed. She hoped that nothing was wrong with one of her brothers or sisters because she would feel terrible knowing that she hadn't checked on them since Franny had been in the hospital. When Dominique didn't hear anything, she thought the phone had somehow hung up. "Hello?"

"Yeah, I'm here. I'm just trying to figure out how to say this," Shanice hesitated.

"Girl, spill the beans and stop holding out, damn," Dominique ordered, getting irritated of her stalling.

"Okay, well some shit went down with Kaleb.

"Oh my God, did something happen to him?" Dominique asked in a panic.

"No, nothing happened *to* him...well, at least not what you're thinking."

"Girl, if you don't stop fucking beating around the damn bush! What the hell happened?" Now upset, Dominique was tired of her friend playing games.

"Alright damn! He supposedly hooked up with some chick." Shanice blurted out.

"Swear to God," Dominique gasped. She hoped that she had heard her wrong.

"I swear."

"What chick?"

Shanice thought for a moment before she responded. "I'm not sure what her name is, but supposedly she just transferred to our school. Her cousin was the one who brought her to the party. Apparently, she and Kaleb started talking and before the night was out, they ended up in the bathroom upstairs. People took pictures and everything," Shanice continued to talk, but Dominique didn't hear anything after she said that Kaleb ended up in the bathroom with the girl. She was truly lost for words and couldn't believe that he would do something like that to her.

"Thanks Nicy, I'll call you back," she said in a panic.

"Wait Nikki—" Shanice started to say, but she was cut off when the phone disconnected.

Immediately, Dominique snatched the receiver back up and started to dial Kaleb's number. She was at the very last digit when Franny was rolled back into the room by the nurse, followed by NiChia.

"They said grandma will definitely be released tomorrow," NiChia said happily. Her expression quickly changed when she noticed the look on Dominique's face. "What's wrong with you, Nikki?"

"Nothing," Dominique lied as she hung up the phone. "I just don't feel good."

"Are you sure baby?" Franny asked. While the nurse helped her back into her bed, she looked over at her granddaughter with worry.

"Yeah, grandma, I'm okay. I'm just going to go outside and get some fresh air because my head is killing me," Dominique told her as she stood up from the chair and walked out of the room.

Chapter Six

In the hallway, Dominique headed to the elevator quickly so that NiChia wouldn't follow behind her. She needed to be alone. Once the elevator doors opened, she pushed the button for the lobby and headed downstairs. On the ground floor, Dominique stepped outside and immediately broke down crying. A few people looked her way before they went back about their business. They all figured that the young girl had gotten some bad news, and each of them decided to leave her with her own thoughts. It took a few minutes before Dominique was able to compose herself. Once she did, she dug into her pocket, pulled out a few quarters, and stormed over to where two payphones sat on the side of the building. Shoving her change into the coin slot, Dominique dialed Kaleb's number. As she waited for it to ring, she hoped that he would tell her that people were mistaken and it hadn't been him with another girl. The phone rang a few times before a male's voice answered.

"Tell me that it isn't true," Dominique cried.

"Who is this?"

"I'm sorry Des, is Kaleb home?" Dominique asked feeling embarrassed. Desmond was Kaleb's best friend, who also lived with them.

"Yeah, hold on a minute. Kaleb!" Desmond yelled.

"Hello?" Kaleb spoke a minute later when he came to the phone.

"I hear you showed yo' ass at the party the other day."

"Nikki listen—"

"No, just tell me that it isn't true."

Kaleb was silent a few seconds before he replied, "I'm sorry."

"Really? That's all you have to say to me?" Dominique wept.

"It wasn't like that Nikki, I swear. Shit just got outta hand. I was drinking and—" he tried to explain.

"You know what, save it!" she yelled. "The last time

we talked, you told me that there were mad chicks trying to fuck with you. I guess you finally decided to take them up on their offer, huh? I hope it was worth it, Kaleb. I'm so done right now; you don't even have a fucking clue!"

"Nikki!" he called out to her. "Just let me explain plea—"

"There ain't shit left for you to explain. I'm done. You can now do what the fuck you've probably been doing all along," Dominique told him with her voice shaking. She hated to think about the possibility that maybe Kaleb had been cheating on her the entire time, and this was the first time that he'd gotten caught. All kinds of thoughts were running through her head. "You know what, fuck you Kaleb! I hope that I never see yo' bitch ass again! I now officially hate you!"

"Nikki—"

Dominique slammed the phone down against the cradle a few times, before dropping it all together. She felt defeated and her heart hurt. She couldn't believe that Kaleb would do something like that to her. With shaky hands, she picked the phone up and hung it back on its cradle before taking a seat on a nearby bench.

With her head inside her hands, she thought about their last conversation. It was the day that they had the fight. Even though she already knew that Kaleb had grown tired of her holding out sex, she never thought in a million years that he would actually go out and get it from someone else. Her thoughts shifted to the fact that she was probably the last to get the memo because everyone at school apparently knew already, especially if there were pictures floating around. This made Kaleb's betrayal even worse because she knew that she had to see those same people day in and day out. Not only that, but she also had to see the bitch that he cheated with. Somehow knowing that he cheated with some random girl made her feel even more like shit because that meant that he didn't even care who he fucked, as long as he got some pussy.

"Now, do you want to tell me whose ass I have to beat?" Dominique heard. When she looked up, she saw NiChia standing over her with her hands propped up on her hips and an angry scowl on her face.

Dominique sighed before she said, "You wouldn't believe it if I told you."

"Try me."

Dominique went on to explain everything that had happed the other day when Kaleb and her got into the argument. She then shared what Shanice had told her, as well as the telephone call that she made a few minutes prior to her coming outside. NiChia was pissed and ready to fuck somebody up. She offered to go over to Kaleb's house and kick his ass for breaking her sister's heart, and although she didn't know who the chick was that he'd cheated with, she was planning on whipping her ass as well. Dominique cried a little longer, while NiChia comforted her, letting her know that everything was going to be alright. Dominique wanted to believe her sister, but at that moment, it hurt way too much. Kaleb had broken her heart, and she knew that she would never be able to forgive him.

Both girls continued to sit outside for a while longer talking. While out there, Dominique came up with the idea of asking Monique if she could live with her grandmother and NiChia. She knew that it was a longshot, but figured if she threatened to tell the police about her mother's assault on her grandmother, Monique would allow her to just go. Dominique knew that her mother was afraid of going to jail, so she was going to use it to her advantage. She didn't know what the future held, but she knew for a fact that she didn't want to go back to the old neighborhood, or her old school. She didn't want the drama and heartache that came along with seeing both Kaleb and his new bitch in the hallway daily. Dominique was through with her now ex-boyfriend and wanted to just be over it, and if that meant moving to another city, she was down. Thoughts of her brothers and sisters clouded her mind. Dominique knew that they would miss her dearly; especially Tiffany. She felt bad for leaving them, but knew that it was something that she had to do for herself.

Not only did she want to get away from Kaleb, but her mother as well. After the fight they'd had in the kitchen the day of Franny's heart attack, Dominique was sure that Monique was still holding onto the grudge she had and couldn't wait until her daughter came back home, so that she could make good on her threat to fuck her up. Even though Monique knew that Dominique could and would whip her ass, that wouldn't stop her from putting her hands on her eldest daughter. This was something that Dominique wasn't looking forward to, not because she was afraid of her mother, but for the fact that she was afraid of what she might do if Monique tried to hit her again. That shit was dead, and if Monique thought for a moment that Dominique was going to sit back and let her smack her around, she had another thing coming.

Thirty minutes later, Dominique was calm enough to go back up to her grandmother's room. Neither of the girls wanted Franny to know what was going on, so they agreed to play along with the lie that Dominique had of not feeling well. It was going to take some acting, but Dominique was up for the challenge. Her grandmother had enough on her plate, and she didn't want to add her problems to the list of things that stressed her out. As Dominique walked side by side with NiChia to the elevator, she promised herself that she wasn't going to shed another tear over Kaleb. He had fucked up by cheating, and losing her was going to be a loss that he was going to have to live with for the rest of his life. She only had a year and a half of school before she was due to graduate and leave Atlanta behind. If she had it her way, she would never see his low down cheating ass ever again.

Chapter Seven

Four and a half years later...

"So, you ain't gone tell me where you were last night, huh Dre?" Dominique asked with her face twisted in disgust.

She stood beside their bed with her arms folded across her chest, staring a hole into the back of her boyfriend's head, as she waited for him to answer her. Even though she knew that she wasn't going to get it, all she wanted was the truth. Dominique's jaws clenched and she rolled her eyes. Her right leg rocked back and forth as she tried her best to calm down, but it was proving harder to do. Deondre was going to make her go there. Annoyed that he was not responding right away, she cocked her head to the side and huffed. She was tired of playing games. She and Deondre 'Dre'

Godby had been together for almost three years, and up until about a few months ago, everything seemed to be fine.

After she swallowed the lump in her throat, Dominique blinked away the tears that were threatening to spill from her eyes. She refused to cry. There was no way in hell that she would allow him to see her hurt behind the dumb shit that he was doing. Dominique hated to consider the fact that Deondre was creeping with another woman, but lately that was all she could think about. It literally made her sick to her stomach when she pictured him touching another female the way he had touched her. It was nauseating to say the least. The numerous unanswered calls that she made to his cellphone and late hours that he had been keeping were taking a toll on her. Although she didn't have any solid proof, Dominique's gut was telling her that her boyfriend was doing her wrong and she was ready to get to the bottom of it.

She watched Deondre from across the room while he acted as if she was tripping about him coming in only a few hours ago. This made her angrier with each passing moment; so angry that she almost acted out her feelings. What Dominique really wanted to do was chuck the glass lamp that sat on top of her nightstand at his head, but she knew better. She had always been taught that if you put your hands on someone, you should be prepared to be hit back. Although Dre had never struck her before, she had seen her fair share of abuse when she was younger between her parents and because of that, she didn't want to open that door between her and her man. Not only that, but she knew that she was no match for the much bigger and stronger male.

"I did tell you where I was. It ain't my fault that you don't believe me," Deondre replied, never once turning around to face her. He couldn't because he was afraid that his deceit would be written all over his face.

"That's because you're a fucking liar!" Dominique screamed. "Why lie though, Dre? If you doing wrong, be a man about it and say that shit. I don't have the time nor the patience to play games with you."

Not bothering to feed into her anger, Deondre walked over to the dresser and pulled out something to wear, hoping that Dominique would just drop the subject, even though he knew that she wouldn't. He didn't feel like arguing with her this early in the morning. What he really wanted to do was sit down and eat breakfast with his family before he had to head to football practice, but by the look of things, he would have to stop somewhere to grab a meal because he knew that Dominique wasn't going to fix him a damn thing.

"Are you ignoring me?" Dominique asked, now standing with her hands on her hips.

"No Nikki, I'm not ignoring you," he answered. "I just don't want to fight. I haven't done anything wrong, but apparently you don't believe me." Deondre turned to face her, while he pulled a pair of jogging pants up around his waist. "What else do you want me to say?"

"You've gotta be kidding me right?" Dominique scoffed. "What I want you to tell me is the fucking truth, that's what! Tell me where you were last night that kept yo' black ass out until the wee hours of the morning."

"I told you I was with the guys. After practice, we went to a bar and had a few drinks. I got fucked up and ended up crashing on Pierre's coach," Deondre lied.

There was no way in hell he could tell her what he was really doing. After practice the day before, Deondre headed over to one of his side chick's house. She cooked him dinner before things got hot and heavy, and he ended up falling asleep. He didn't plan on spending the night over there, but that's how it ended up happening. Deondre had never stayed out all night before, so he was hoping that Dominique would believe his lie and chalk it up to an honest mistake. The lie still made her mad, but much less upset than what would happen if the truth was revealed. It was no secret that his girlfriend was a firecracker who didn't take shit from anyone; him included. Had Dominique known the truth, shit would have gotten real and he couldn't take that chance. Deondre felt a little better knowing that his Pierre would back his story.

"So, you mean to tell me that the entire time you were out *drinking with the guys*," Dominique used her fingers to make air quotes, "you didn't notice that I was calling? Or better yet, you could not once pick up your fucking phone and call me back because you ain't finna tell me that you didn't see all of those missed called."

Deondre stood there for a second before he answered her question. She had called his phone quite a few times but because he was preoccupied, he didn't even bother to answer. He also knew that if he had, the person he was with would have caught an attitude and that would have ruined the mood. Snatching up his jeans off of the floor, Deondre rummaged through the pockets. He pulled out his wallet and a few crumbled up bills, but no cellphone. Unbeknownst to Dominique, Deondre knew that his phone was in the glove apartment of his truck. He put it there right before he came into the house a few hours ago because he knew that she would bring up calling him.

"Damn, baby," he sighed. "I must have either left it in the locker or in my gym bag that's in the trunk after I left practice," he lied. "I'm sorry."

"You're so full of shit Dre, I swear." Dominique shook her head and took a seat on the edge of the bed. "I don't believe that bullshit you're feeding me, but I'm gone let you have it this time. Just know that the truth will come to light one day, and if you've been doing me dirty like I suspect, then I'll find out sooner or later. I'm not going to play the fool, Dre. I'll leave yo' mutha'fucking ass high and dry before I do," she promised. "And that's something that you betta believe."

"See, why do you always gotta say shit like that?"

Deondre asked, as he made his way over to where she was sitting. Once he was close enough, he reached out and grabbed her, pulling her up toward him. "Don't you know I love you, girl?"

"Uh huh." She swatted his hands away and returned to her seat on the bed. "That's always your favorite line when you know you've fucked up. Apparently, you don't love me enough because yo' ass ain't never home. You always got somewhere to be, leaving me at home. I'm really getting tired of this shit, Dre. If I want to lie in bed alone, I can be by my damn self," Dominique told him. "Yo' ass think you slick though, but you not. I know that you've been up to no good."

"I promise, I ain't doing shit baby," Deondre assured her. "It's me and you until the end of time. You know that, right?"

"Whatever Dre," Dominique mumbled. Her heart wanted to believe everything that he was saying, but her gut was telling her that he was full of shit.

"I'm serious. I can't really tell you just yet, but shit is about to get real for your man. I know I've been M.I.A for a little while and out of touch, but it'll all make sense in a few. I promise. When it does, I don't want anyone else in the world by my side other than you." Deondre reached out and grabbed her once again. When he pulled her close, he was glad to see that she did resist this time. "We're heading straight to the top. Just bear with me, baby."

Dominique allowed herself to fall into his embrace. She sighed as her small frame was completely engulfed by his large arms. Standing at a mere five-foot-two and a hundred and twenty-five pounds, she looked like a child compared to Deondre's much larger stature. Her man was six-feet-two inches tall, and well over two hundred pounds of solid muscle that she absolutely loved. Not only was he built, but Deondre was also a very handsome man. His skin tone was the perfect shade of mocha, and his deep dark brown eyes were so intoxicating, she found herself lost in them at times. Dominique loved Deondre, and even though she had a feeling that he was up to no good, she prayed for the best and wanted nothing more than for her family to stay together.

"I gotta go to practice but soon, I'll be able to explain everything. You're going to love it," Deondre told her before he placed a gentle kiss on her forehead.

"See what I mean. You just got here, and you're already about to leave back out," Dominique pouted.

"You know I gotta go to practice baby."

"I know, but damn," she groaned. "You know what, never mind. Just go do your thing."

"Come on, don't act like that."

Although Deondre towered over her, he was nothing but a big teddy bear when it came to Dominique. He may have strayed, but anyone who knew him knew that there wasn't a woman alive that could make him leave Dominique. What he'd said to her was the absolute truth. There was no one else in the world that he wanted by his side when he made it to the top, other than her. That was why he was looking forward to everything he worked so hard for to pay off. Deondre hadn't told Dominique yet, but he had gotten some wonderful news and planned to share the information with her as soon as he got word that everything was a go. He also planned to ask her to marry him, once everything was official. Deondre wanted to show Dominique just how much he appreciated her for being down with him from the very start.

Dominique met Deondre through Shanice the summer of her freshmen year in high school. They were at a barbeque for Shanice's cousin, Pierre, when she introduced Deondre as a close family friend. After a quick exchange of hellos, they both went about their business, not running into each other again until Dominique's first week of college, when she walked into her biology class. At first, she didn't know where she knew Deondre from, but after he introduced himself to her again, she recalled them meeting. She even remembered Shanice saying how sexy he was; which was true. While Dominique was glad to see a familiar face at her new school, she and Deondre didn't say much to one another, even though she sat directly in front of him.

From the first time he'd laid eyes on her, Deondre had always thought that Dominique was cute, and now that they were at the same school, he wanted to get to know her better. To him, she was nothing like the other girls that he'd come across. Where they were flashy and wanted to be seen all of the time, Dominique was more low-key. They wore tons of make-up, long hair weave, and flashy clothes, while her pretty face was always bare, except for a coat of shiny lip gloss, her hair was worn in natural styles, and her wardrobe was simple. Dominique opted for jeans, a t-shirt, and tennis shoes; while skin tight jeans, short skirts, and hi-heels were what clothed the other chicks day in and day out. Deondre loved the fact that Dominique was different and even though he could tell that she didn't have a lot of money, she fooled most with her keen sense in fashion. Dominique could throw the cheapest outfit together and make it look designer. After coming up with a plan to get close to her, Deondre asked the biology teacher to pair them for a project together.

He and Dominique met at the library a few times. They spoke briefly about the project, but not much about anything else. Afterwards, they began to hang out because neither of them knew a lot of people at school. Things started out slow between the two of them, but Deondre didn't care, as long as he was a part of her life, no matter how small. Dominique wasn't trying to spend too much time with him because she figured that Shanice liked him, even though Deondre told her that she was like a little cousin to him. Everything changed when Dominique found out that she hadn't gotten the loan money that she'd counted on. Since she was only seventeen and still a dependent of her mother, the FAFSA had to calculate Monique's income to determine her financial aid and loan amount.

Knowing what her daughter needed, Monique decided to be spiteful and didn't send in her information like Dominique asked. She was still upset that her daughter had moved in with her grandmother and was trying to make her pay for leaving her to tend to all of her kids. As a result of Monique's pettiness, Dominique lost her loan and financial aid money for that year. Once that happened, Dominique couldn't afford to continue living in her dorm room. The little money that she made at her part-time job was only enough to cover her books, food, and personal needs. This devastated Dominique because she knew that when that semester was over, she would have to drop out of school and move back home to her grandmother's house.

When Dominique showed up at Deondre's apartment with tears in her eyes, he comforted her before he told her that she was more than welcome to move into his two-bedroom apartment with him. Since his uncle, who had raised him after his father was sent to prison for drug trafficking, was a well-known business owner with more money than he could count, Deondre didn't have to worry about money. All that was asked of him was to attend school and make something of himself; which he was doing. While he did that, his uncle made sure that he had everything he wanted and more. With a healthy monthly allowance, Deondre really didn't have any worries.

At first, Dominique turned him down. She didn't want to become dependent on a guy that she barely even knew. That was until her days in her dorm began to get shorter and shorter. By then, she realized that either she move in with Deondre, or head back home and sign up at community college. Dominique didn't want to do that, so she finally accepted Deondre's invitation and he helped her move her stuff over to his apartment. Since it wasn't like he was exactly a stranger on the street, she felt comfortable enough to not second guess it.

For months, everything was the same. Deondre slept in his room, and Dominique slept in hers. They hung out a lot more because most of the time, they were both at home. They did things like study together and have movie nights, which was fun for Dominique, who loved a good film. One late night, after receiving a call from his uncle, Deondre broke down. He had found out that his father had been killed during a riot in prison. As he cried in his bedroom, Dominique heard him and went in to see what was going on. When he explained everything to her, she felt bad for her friend and tried to console him as best she could. Dominique couldn't imagine what Deondre was going through and knew that if the shoe was over the other foot and something had happened to her dad, she would be devastated as well. That night, one thing led to another and they ended up sleeping together. Dominique didn't know if it happened because she was emotional about her own father, or if it was really something that she'd wanted all along. Whatever the case was, she didn't beat herself up too much about it because the deed had already been done.

Soon after that night, they ended up making it official and became a couple. Deondre helped Dominique as much as he could with everything she needed, and she convinced him to go after his dream to become a professional football player. She sat in the bleachers the day of Deondre's very first practice and was just as excited as he was when he found out that he made the team. Apparently he was so good that within that first year, he was known as the running back that everyone had their eye on. Since then, numerous scouts from other schools had approached him about transferring and joining their teams, but he always shot them down, choosing to stay at Middle Georgia State University with Dominique. Deondre was on his way to the big leagues, and it wouldn't have been possible without Dominique giving him the push that he needed. That was one of the reasons why Deondre loved her so much and promised to always take care of her.

"I'll come home early later, and we can do something together," Deondre told Dominique, still looking down at her.

"Whatever Dre. Just go do whatever it is that you have plans on doing," Dominique retorted. The sound of whining coming from the other side of the apartment got her attention. "Bye," she told him, as she rushed out of their bedroom.

Quickly, she made her way across the hall. Once she

entered the brightly colored room, Dominique smiled when she saw her two year old son, Deondre Jr., who everyone called DJ, standing up in his crib. As soon as his eyes landed on her, he stopped whining and began to excitedly bounce up and down on his little legs, happy to see his mommy.

"What's wrong with my baby?" Dominique asked walking over towards him.

"Mommy!" DJ yelled. He was now smiling.

He was teething, so slobber dribbled down his chin and onto the all-white onesie he wore. Dominique looked at her son and made a funny face before she bent down and picked him up, placing him on her hip. With her thumb, she wiped away the tears that were present before kissing on his chubby cheeks. DJ giggled and kicked his feet as he attempted to get away from his mother when she started to tickle him up under his neck.

"How is daddy's big boy?" Deondre said walking into the room.

Dominique smacked her lips, but didn't say anything. She was in a happy place with her son and wasn't going to let Deondre's stupid ass ruin her mood.

"Daddy has to go. I'll see you when I get home," Deondre said, as if DJ actually knew what the hell he was talking about. He leaned in and placed a kiss on the top of his son's head, before he attempted to mash his lips against Dominique's.

"Bye Dre," she said with her hand in front of her face. She still didn't know where he had been the night before and didn't want his lips to be anywhere near hers.

Deondre took a step back, shook his head, and turned to walk away.

"I know you're mad right now, but I love you, Nikki," he told her.

When she didn't reply, he disappeared through the door and down the stairs. It wasn't long after when Dominique heard the front door open and close. With DJ propped on her hip, she exited the room and headed downstairs to the kitchen to prepare the two of them something to eat. Downstairs, she placed DJ in his highchair and pulled out everything that she needed to make them a hearty meal. While Dominique cooked, she continued to get a nagging feeling that Deondre wasn't telling her the truth. Things weren't adding up, and she wanted to get to the bottom of it. Although she loved the cushy lifestyle she lived, she would move in with her grandmother in a heartbeat before she allowed him to think that it was okay for him to cheat and treat her like shit. Dominique had left one man for straying, and she wasn't above doing it again.

Picking up the house phone from its base, she dialed her best friend's number.

"What you doing, bitch?" she asked, as soon as Shanice answered.

"Shit, just sitting here watching TV. What you doing?"

"Sitting here trying to figure out what the hell Dre's been up to."

"Why you say that?" Shanice questioned, rolling her eyes.

"Girl, he didn't come home last night. Then he gone try to make me believe that he went out drinking with his friends and ended up falling asleep on Pierre's couch." Dominique smacked her lips. "I swear he thinks I'm a fool."

"So, he didn't come home *at all* last night?"

"Nope, he walked in the door around six in the

morning, and left right back out a minute ago."

"That bitch," Shanice whispered.

"What you say?" Dominique asked with her ear pushed closer to the phone.

"Girl, nothing. I was just thinking that that's fucked up," Shanice recovered, glad that her friend hadn't heard her. "So, what did you do?" she asked even though she didn't care.

Dominique went on to tell her friend everything else that had happened before Deondre left out for practice. Shanice commented negatively like she always did, telling Dominique to leave Deondre alone and find her someone who would treat her better. Dominique ignored her because she figured that her friend didn't have a lot of room to talk. Shanice didn't even have a man that wanted to claim her, so her opinions about what Dominique did with her baby daddy didn't matter much. It's kind of hard to take someone's relationship advice, when they've never been in a true relationship.

"I'm about to feed my baby and when I'm finished, I'm going to get us both dressed. We're going to drive up there. I miss London anyway," Dominique said, referring to her God-child, which was Shanice's three year old daughter.

"No!" Shanice yelled in a panic, before softening her voice. "Lamar is about to come over here to see us. I'll call you when he leaves, okay?"

"Humph, okay. Just call me later, I'm about to find something to do."

Dominique hung up the phone thinking to herself that Shanice had lost her damn mind. Here she was giving her advice on what she should do with her man, and she was one of the biggest fools of them all. Lamar was Shanice's baby daddy, who only came around when it was convenient for him. Although Dominique had never officially met the dude, she knew that he wasn't shit and only came and went as he pleased because Shanice allowed him to. Dominique couldn't understand why her friend was so weak for a dude who was barely around and when he did pop up, he didn't stay for long. Shanice was a pretty girl and could have her pick of the litter, but for some reason, she chose him.

Lamar was something like a ghost because no one other than Shanice had actually seen him. Dominique wondered why things about him were always so secretive, especially when she shared every part of her life with her best friend. It kind of hurt her feelings to know that Shanice didn't trust her enough to share that information with her. Dominique had never even seen a picture of London's daddy or knew what his last name was. Shanice only referred to him as Lamar, so that's all everybody knew. While Dominique wanted to know the details about her friend's child's father for her own sake, she didn't want to push the issue and figured that when Shanice was ready to talk, she would.

Dominique pushed the thoughts of Shanice and her love life to the back of her mind. She had bigger fish to fry and worrying about who her friend was fucking was not one of them. It didn't really concern her, in her opinion. No, what she needed to worry about was what her own man was getting into, or better yet, *who* he was getting into. Deondre had made her think that everything he was doing was a part of some great thing he had going on, and even though Dominique wanted to believe it, she knew better. Boo boo the fool was not written on her forehead, so Deondre had better come with something better than just falling asleep on somebody's couch because she didn't believe that shit at all. Dominique figured that she would find out what her man was up to soon enough, and if she did catch wind that Deondre was fucking around, she wasn't just going to leave him, she was going to show him that two could play that game. If her heart was fucked up, his was going to be too.

Chapter Eight

As soon as Shanice hung up with Dominique, she immediately picked her phone back up and dialed another number. While the phone rang, she paced back and forth across her carpeted floor. She was livid after hearing the news that she heard. *That bastard has a lot of fucking nerves,* she thought to herself. *He seriously got me fucked up.* The line rang a few more times before it rolled over to the voicemail. There was no way that Shanice was leaving a message as mad as she was, so she mashed the end button before hitting redial. This went on for the next ten minutes before the person she was calling finally answered.

"Why the hell are you calling my phone back to back like that for?" he asked irritated. "I hope it's important. Is something wrong with my daughter or something?"

"Where the fuck was you at last night?" Shanice yelled into the receiver. She didn't give a damn what he was talking about, she wanted answers.

He exhaled loudly. "Man, what the hell you tripping about now?" Deondre asked. He wasn't in the mood to argue with her right then. He had just gotten to practice and didn't have the time.

"Don't fucking play with me, Dre! I've already talked to Nikki and she told me that yo' ass didn't come home until early this morning. You weren't with me, so who in the fuck were you with last night?"

"First off, you need to calm the fuck down and stop yelling at me like a fucking child or something!" Deondre barked. "Secondly, don't call me telling me what you heard from somebody else."

"So, that's all you have to say for yourself?"

"Hell yeah! That's all I gotta say. Nicy, you ain't my woman. What part of that don't you understand?"

"I ain't gotta be ya fucking woman, Dre. I'm the mother of your child, so the least you can do is tell me something," she told him seriously. "You ain't gone keep fucking me while you out here fucking other bitches. I already gotta share you with Nikki, but I'll be damn if I share you with all these other hoes too."

"Shut the fuck up Nicy with all that whining and shit because you giving me a fucking headache. You act like you my baby momma by choice. Don't forget you were the one who hopped on my dick, so please stop acting like I came after you. You wanted to fuck me, remember? Not only that, but you do know that you ain't gotta keep fucking with me. You're free to leave whenever you want. I ain't holding ya ass hostage."

"Whatever Dre."

"Whatever my ass. Don't get all short with your answers now. A minute ago, you were yelling and acting a fucking fool on the phone. Wanna call me back to back and shit, just to tell me what you heard. I ain't got time for all that shit, Nicy. Just tell me what the hell you want from me?"

"You know what I want, Dre?" Shanice asked. "I want you to stop lying to me all the fucking time. I want you to stop being so damn disrespectful towards me when you get caught out here, and I want you to treat me like you treat that bitch!" Shanice screamed.

"Watch your fucking mouth dammit!" Deondre

snarled.

"See what I mean. I can't say anything about your precious Nikki without you jumping down my throat. Why do you always gotta act like that towards me?" By now, Shanice was crying. "What do I have to do for you to treat me like I treat you?"

"This is the shit I be talking about," Deondre snarled. "All that crying and shit is a fucking turn off. You knew what it was before hand, so why are you so bent on changing shit that you knew wasn't going to change in the first place? Put on your big girl panties and grow the fuck up, Nicy! I swear, sometimes you're a pain in my ass!"

"I bet you don't say shit like that to Nikki," Shanice complained. Her feelings were hurt and she was tired of him speaking to her as if she didn't matter to him.

"Why do you always gotta bring her up? You right though because I sure the fuck don't talk to her like this because she doesn't get on my fucking nerves like you do," Deondre admitted, losing his patience. He was getting tired of Shanice and all her fucking whining.

"I'm just saying, you don't talk to her—"

"See, that's your problem. You don't know when to

shut the fuck up! Plus, you're too busy worried about Nikki and what we got going on, when truthfully, it ain't none of ya business," he explained.

Deondre was tired of having the same conversation with Shanice over and over again. He felt bad for flipping on her the way he was, but he couldn't help himself. Dominique had already busted his balls just a few hours ago, and now he had to deal with the same thing from her. Deondre was starting to wonder if it was worth it to keep fucking with her. If the side chick was nagging you just as much as the main chick, what was the point of having her around?

"You sound stupid saying that. She's my bestfr—"

"You could've fooled the hell outta me!" He laughed, cutting her sentence short. "She's your best friend, yet you're on the phone calling yourself checking *her man* about fucking someone *other than you*," Deondre continued to crack up at how dumb she sounded.

"You can talk all the shit you want, but you ain't no damn better, Dre. Let's not forget that you're just as guilty as I am," Shanice pointed out. "While you talking shit, I'm sure you really don't want me to show my ass because I will. I'll tell everything, even all the other shit that you don't want anyone to know. You just keep fucking with me if you want to," she threatened. "I don't think Nikki would be too happy to find out that her baby daddy was mine's first, among other things."

"Bitch please!" Deondre boomed. "You can play crazy if you want to, but you and I both know that you ain't stupid enough to do no shit like that. You can keep your threats because I ain't worried," Deondre replied, calling her on her bullshit, even though he prayed that that's all it was. "Not only would Nikki beat the brakes off yo' ass and cut you off, but I'll send some bitches your way that will make you regret the day that you ever fucked with me. I have some words of advice for you. Stop talking crazy while you're ahead because you're really starting to piss me off!" Deondre told her. "I'm busy at practice right now. Don't call me on this bullshit no more!"

"Damn nigga. Who the hell you going off on?" a male voice asked in the background.

"Nobody. Just some dumb ass girl." Shanice heard Deondre say right before the phone disconnected.

Shanice was so mad that she threw her phone

across the room. It bounced off the wall and fell to the floor, with the back and battery sliding underneath the couch. Her outburst scared London, who immediately burst into tears. Irritated, Shanice walked over to her crying toddler and snatched her up by her arm. This made London cry harder as she stared at her mother with a terrified look on her face. Shanice immediately felt bad for taking out her frustrations on her child and rubbed her arm in an attempt to make it feel better.

"Mommy's sorry, baby. I didn't mean it."

When her usually talkative daughter didn't say anything in return, Shanice knew that it was because she was still afraid of what she might have done. In all honesty, London had a right to be scared. It wasn't like that had been the first time that Shanice had struck her after getting mad at her father. Poor little London had had her fair share of bumps and bruises behind her mother's anger, and it was all because Shanice couldn't physically make Deondre feel her wrath. The last time it happened, London walked around with a black eye for more than a week. Of course, Shanice told Deondre that she'd ran into the corner of the end table while playing around the house because she knew that, although

Deondre didn't claim her as his woman, he loved his daughter to death and if he had even thought that she was putting her hands on her, Shanice would have gotten the ass whipping of a lifetime.

It took a few moments before London began to slack up with her crying and it was only because Shanice leaned down and kissed the part of her arm where it hurt. Just like Shanice, London loved attention. Even at her young age, she knew to do things just when she knew that someone was watching. London could be dancing around the house. If she caught someone looking and smiling, she would do it over and over again, just so she would keep whoever it was watching her. So, when Shanice kissed her boo-boo, she sucked it all up and enjoyed her mother's love. It was cute and harmless because she was young, but if she grew up to be anything like her mother, it would just be sad.

Shanice looked at her daughter with sad eyes. She was truly sorry for snatching her baby up the way that she had. It wasn't London's fault that her daddy was acting like an asshole who didn't know how to talk properly to her mother. With her toddler now placed on her hip, she bounced London up and down until she got a smile out of her. This let Shanice know that there had been no damage done and that all was forgiven. Shanice went into the kitchen to get London a small bag of chips and a juice, before she sat her on the couch with her snacks. After switching the channels of the TV for a minute, she was glad to see that *Dora The Explorer* was on. *This will keep her busy for a while,* Shanice reasoned.

"Thank you, Mommy." London said with her eyes locked on the television.

"You're welcome, baby."

Now that her daughter was happy, Shanice's mind drifted over to Deondre. She thought about all of the nasty things that he had said to her. He sat on that phone and acted like she didn't have a right to be upset about him possibly sleeping with other women. *He's got life fucked up.* The killer was the fact that he tried to carry her by reminding her that she wasn't his woman. No, she wasn't his woman like he'd said, but he damn sure acted like it when they were together. Although Shanice was mad, she knew that Deondre was just talking shit. This wasn't the first time that he had said hurtful things like that. He did it often and most of the time, it was after he had gotten caught up; which had been more than a dozen times.

Shanice rolled her eyes when she thought about how predictable Deondre was. He used that 'You're not my woman' thing just to get his ass out of hot water. He never brought the shit up when he was fucking her raw every chance he got. Although it wasn't the least bit funny, Shanice couldn't help but to laugh because Deondre was full of shit. He never said no shit like that when he thought that she was fucking around with another dude. Nah, he would hit, choke, and threaten to beat the shit out of her if he even had the thought that she was thinking about finding someone else.

Maybe that's not a bad idea, she reasoned. *I should find me someone who knows how to talk to a woman and not be so damn disrespectful.* There was no reason for Deondre to talk to her the way he had. Shanice knew that she should have been used to it, but she wasn't. It wasn't the first time that he'd called her bitches and gotten loud, in fact, he did it at least once a week. It made Shanice mad to hear him speak to her that way, when he barely even raised his voice at Dominique. She didn't understand why he treated her best friend like a princess, when all she did was curse him out. Dominique yelled at Deondre about *everything*, and all he did in return was apologize and find some way to make her smile. Shanice knew that if she yelled half as much as Dominique did, he would have smacked her in the mouth and told her to shut the fuck up. She knew this because whenever she said *anything* out of pocket, he called her every name in the book and told her that if she didn't like it, she could leave me alone, even though he knew she wouldn't,

This was unfair to Shanice, who only wanted Deondre to be honest about who he was fucking around with. That would give her a chance to protect herself and make him use condoms, instead of allowing him to have intercourse with her without one. There were way too many diseases out there, and Shanice didn't want to catch any. Plus, she already had to share him with Dominique; which was exhausting enough. Just having to sit on the phone having to listen to her best friend talk about all of the things that she and Deondre did on a day to day basis made Shanice sick. She wanted so bad to tell her Dominique *'who fucking cares'* but she knew better. Instead, she just sat there and listened, all while wishing that she could just burst her bubble with the fact that she was fucking him too.

Shanice's silence wasn't for the sake of Dominique, but more for Deondre. She knew that if she said anything about them being together, he would cut her off, and that was something that she knew she couldn't live with. Shanice loved Deondre with everything in her. So much so that she knew that she loved him more than Dominique did. Deondre was nothing but a savior for Dominique, and nothing more. Everything she had was because of him and without him, she was nothing. While Dominique depended on Deondre to survive, Shanice was good without anything he gave her. Her parents made sure that she wanted for nothing, even in her adult years. Due to this, everything that Deondre gave her went either to their daughter or in her bank account. Shanice had everything else she needed; everything except him.

Had it not been for her so-called "best friend" he would have been hers from the very beginning. Deondre had been friends with her cousin, Pierre, for as long as she could remember. He used to come to all of the family functions, and every time she saw him, she knew that he was who she wanted to be her man. Shanice started to talk to Deondre more frequently when he was around and every chance she got, she flirted. She would put on her cutest outfits, tell him how good he looked, or make his plate whenever it was time to eat. Still, Deondre never showed any interest at all.

By the time Shanice was in the eleventh grade, she had moved on to other things. She had gotten bored with chasing after Deondre. That was around the time that Dominique had moved away to live with her grandmother and with her gone, Shanice had officially become one of the most popular girls at school. All of the boys flocked to her like bees to honey and she loved it. The next time Shanice saw Deondre was at her aunt's birthday party. He walked in with a gift in his hand, and as soon as he saw Shanice, he smiled and waved. She, in turn, rolled her eyes and walked away. This time, she didn't have any plans on striking up a conversation with Deondre because she was over it. After thinking about how he had been brushing her off, Shanice came to the conclusion that he had to have been gay. She thought about the fact that she had never seen Deondre with a girl. Add in the fact that her family thought that her cousin Pierre was gay, so it made sense that he was as well. Soon, Deondre became nothing but a memory. That was until he popped back up again.

When Dominique called Shanice and told her that she had just seen Deondre in her biology class, Shanice pretended to be happy, even though she didn't give a shit. Soon after, she found out that they were study buddies, but still didn't care at all. A few months in was when Dominique started to like Deondre, so she called Shanice and asked her if she was okay with them possibly dating because she knew that she had a crush on him in the past. Still believing Deondre was gay, Shanice told Dominique that it was cool if they hooked up, knowing that that would never happen. Her exact words were, '*Go ahead girl, he's family to me.*' It wasn't until Dominique called all giddy and shit and explained that they had officially become a couple that Shanice realized that Dondre wasn't gay at all. As she listened to Dominique tell her about their very first sexual experience, Shanice's heart broke. She immediately got off the phone and cried for an hour straight.

Shanice couldn't figure out why Deondre hadn't

liked her. She was beautiful, dressed nice, and was the cousin of his best friend. He already knew that she came from a good family because he was around them all the time. It only made sense that he would have wanted to be with her. Out of all the people in the word, the person that he chose to be with was her best friend. Deondre looked over her for a girl who wore her own nappy ass hair, dressed in thrift store clothing, and came from a fucked up dysfunctional home; the same person that Shanice had grown tired of coming in second place to.

Shanice couldn't' figure out what he had seen in her. Although Dominique had a nice 'cute little' body, it was nothing compared to Shanice's much curvier figure. While Dominique had a slim build, small breasts, and medium sized butt, Shanice had D cups, thick thighs, and a fat ass. In Shanice's mind, she had everything that any man could ever want, so she wasn't sure why Deondre didn't see that. Knowing that Dominique had conquered something that she wanted, Shanice promised herself that she was going to fuck up their so-called happy relationship. If she couldn't have Deondre, Dominique wasn't going to have him either.

A few months later, Shanice got her chance. It was her parents' twentieth anniversary, and she knew that all of her family would be in attendance. Just to make sure that Deondre was going to be there, she called Pierre, who confirmed that they were both coming. Once she got her answer, she came up with her plan. Later that night, while everyone was laughing, drinking, and having a good old time in her parents' backyard, she walked up to Deondre and struck up a conversation. They talked for a few minutes about nothing, until he brought up Dominique. Since Shanice wasn't trying to hear anything about their relationship, she excused herself to put her plan into motion.

A few minutes later, Shanice approached him with two drinks in her hand. With a smile on her face, she handed him one of the drinks and kept one for herself. Not thinking anything of it, Deondre took the cup and downed the drink before he picked their conversation right back, with Dominique being the topic. Shanice used the fact that the music was playing to act like she really couldn't really hear anything that he was saying, so they took their conversation into the house. While inside her living room, Deondre bragged on his relationship with her best friend, Shanice was waiting patiently for the two crushed up Ambien's that she had stolen from her mother's medicine cabinet to kick in. She knew that they took anywhere from twenty to forty-five minutes to kick in, so she kept him talking.

A half hour later, Deondre's speech started to slur. When he shook his head a few times, Shanice knew that it was time to take action. She helped him to stand up and guided him to her bedroom, telling him that she was going to lay him down. As soon as they crossed the threshold of her room, she closed and locked the door. After pushing Deondre backwards onto her bed, she slowly climbed on top of him and kissed him in the mouth. Seeing as though he wasn't really into it, she moved down and began to undress him. Shanice was surprised that his penis wasn't bigger, since he was such a stocky guy, but she didn't care because she was about to do something that she had dreamed about for years.

Taking his dick into her mouth, she sucked on it for a few moments, which brought a few moans from the back of Deondre's throat. Although he was half asleep, the pleasure that she was giving him did not go unnoticed. With his penis now hard, Shanice climbed on top of him and took what she wanted. She was only able to ride him for about ten minutes before he came. Since he wasn't wearing a condom, his seeds filled her womb. Shanice took advantage of him a few more times before she rolled him over and snuggled in to bed beside him.

A few hours later, Deondre jumped up out of her bed. He couldn't believe that he had not only slept with his friend's little cousin, but she was also his girl's best friend. He begged Shanice not to say anything to Dominique, but she said that she wouldn't feel right keeping a secret like that her from friend. Shanice told him that the only way that she would keep it a secret was if they continued to fuck around on the low. At first, Deondre thought that she had lost her damn mind, but after thinking it over, he realized that it may not be as bad as he thought. He could keep his girlfriend, while having his secret pussy on the side.

It wasn't even a month later when Shanice found out that she was pregnant by Deondre. When she told him, he almost had a heart attack. He didn't know what he would do and definitely didn't want Dominique to find out. He promised Shanice to be there for her and the baby, as well as give her a set amount of money each month. Shanice only agreed, because she figured that before long Deondre would get tired of Dominique, and then he and she could be exclusive. It had been more than 3 years and she was still stuck in the background.

There was no doubt in Shanice's mind that Dominique would be crushed if she found out about her and Deondre messing around. It would be even worse to find out that her very own God-daughter was actually her son's older sister. Shanice laughed when she thought about just how heartbroken Dominique would be. She would finally see that she isn't as special as she thought she was. Dominique thought that since she had DJ, she was the only one going to eat when Deondre became a big time professional football player. What she didn't know was that Shanice was hungry too, and having London make sure that she had a plate as well.

Shanice was tired of her best friend getting everything that she wanted first. It all started with Kaleb. Dominique knew that she was the first one to see him. Shanice had told Dominique on several occasions that Kaleb was cute, but like always, that didn't stop Dominique from going after him and making him her boyfriend. Since then, Shanice secretly hated Dominique. The only reason she kept her around was to keep tabs on her. It was the like the saying, *keep your friends close and your enemies closer,* because that's exactly what Shanice was doing. Dominique may have thought that she had a best friend, but what she didn't know was that Shanice was just waiting for the chance to snatch everything that she believed she deserved away from her.

Chapter Nine

The beautiful sound of a smooth melody coming from the bathroom caused Kaleb's eyes to flutter open. He continued to lie in bed staring at the ceiling for a few more moments, as he listened to the melodic sound serenading him as if she was singing her ballad just for him. Now fully awake, he stretched his arms high above his head and glanced at the clock beside him. It was a little after nine a.m., and even though it was still rather early, Kaleb didn't mean to sleep as long as he did. He had plans today and knew that the earlier he got them done, the more time he had to chill later. With a grunt, he forced himself into an upright position, tossed the covers off of his body, and stood up. Kaleb looked down and laughed when he saw that his manhood was standing at attention through the briefs that he wore. There was no doubt what he needed.

Making his way toward the open bathroom entrance, he stepped out of his underwear along the way. The glass shower door was fogged from the steam, making it hard for him to see inside. That was fine with Kaleb because he knew the body behind the door like the back of his hand and even with his eyes closed he could find his way around with no problem.

"I don't wanna stop just because you feel so good inside of my love. I'm not gonna stop no, no, no, I want you. All I wanna say is..." the angelic voice belted out. "Anytime and anyplace, I don't care who's around."

The chorus of, *Anytime, Anyplace* by Janet Jackson rolled off her tongue in such a perfect harmony that one would believe that the song had been written especially for her. Kaleb grabbed the door handle and stepped inside the shower, slowly closing it behind him. The smell of the fruity shampoo that she had used immediately invaded his nostrils. Not moving, he just stood there, unbeknownst to her, and took in her beauty. Her long wavy hair was wet and lathered with shampoo. It hung down her back, stopping just above her behind. She didn't have one of those ghetto booty's that he was used to, but it fit her tall and slender frame perfectly. Just the sight of her nakedness caused his member to jump in anticipation of being inside her. He quickly closed the space between the two of them and pressed his hardness up against her naked body.

"Oh my God, Kaleb, you scared me!" Tiera screamed when she turned around. Playfully, she smacked her hand against his chest and smiled.

"You were in here jamming, so you didn't hear me calling your name," he fibbed, moving his body even closer to hers.

"I know. I was in a zone," she snickered. "I heard it on satellite radio on my way in, and it's been stuck in my head ever since." When Tiera felt his hands reach around and cup her ass, she cocked her head to the side and asked, "Did you miss me?"

Kaleb groaned before he replied, "Come on Te-Te, you know I did—"

Before he had a chance to get the last word completely out, Tiera smashed her lips against his. Her tongue snaked around inside his mouth hungrily. It had been three weeks since she had seen her man in the flesh because she had been in New York for a modeling gig. They had FaceTimed daily, but that wasn't the same or enough, in her opinion. Now that Tiera was back, she was ready to make up for lost time. With her mind on getting down to business, she broke their kiss and got down on her knees. The shower water rained down on top of her, leaving a trail of a soapy mixture from her head to the drain. That didn't bother Tiera though, because she had a job to do.

Kaleb let out a satisfying moan when she wrapped her lips around his thick rod. Without using her hands, Tiera glided it into her warm mouth and began to bob her head up and down on it.

"Shhhhiiiit," Kaleb moaned.

Lost in the sensation, he rested his back against the shower wall and grabbed a handful of her soaked hair. Kaleb watched as his dick slid back and forth out of her pink lips. His knees buckled when she began to deep throat him, as if his size and girth were nothing to her. *I taught her well,* he thought to himself. Tiera continued with her oral assault. Each passing minute brought Kaleb closer and closer to the point of no return. When she felt his penis began to pulsate, she quickly removed it from her mouth and stood up. It wasn't that Tiera was a stranger to swallowing because she'd done it often; it was just that she was ready to feel him inside her.

Now taking the lead, Kaleb spun her around and placed her up against the shower walls face first. Her small perky breasts smashed against the cool glass, giving her nipples a chilling sensation that she enjoyed. Tiera responded by standing on her tippy toes and pushing her butt towards him. With his left hand, Kaleb placed his throbbing penis outside her moist wet slit and guided himself in inch by inch, until he was completely inside her. Tiera gasped and closed her eyes. She loved how he filled her special place up to capacity. Neither of the two moved, as they both enjoyed the feel of one another. Tiera's tight fit was enough to take Kaleb all the way over the edge, but he refocused his mind elsewhere and held it in. Even though he knew that this would be a quickie, he wanted to enjoy her for as long as he could, before it was time for him to head out for business.

A grunt escaped Kaleb's lips when she rocked his hips slightly. It was then that he felt the muscles inside her warm tunnel tighten around him. Tiera had been going hard on her Kegels the entire time she was gone, so when she squeezed down on his dick, it appeared as if she was trying to suck the life out of it. She knew that Kaleb couldn't control himself when she did that, and she wanted nothing more than to please him. Taking control, he gripped her hips and pushed into her with so much force, she temporarily lost her balance. As she struggled to stand upright, Tiera reached and grabbed ahold of the towel holder. Now that she had something to give her more stability, she looked back at Kaleb with a lustful grin.

"God, I've missed you so much," she breathed, throwing her head back.

"Did you miss me, or did you miss this dick?" Kaleb asked while he continued to slide in and out of her at a steady pace.

"Ummm," Tiera moaned. "I've missed you...ahhh shit! I've missed you both!"

She arched her back even more and began to push herself off of the shower wall with her free hand, while still holding on to the towel holder with the other. Each time her body slammed into his, Kaleb felt himself going deeper and deeper, until his dick was hitting the bottom of her pussy. He knew it was only a matter of time before he lost it, so he quickly pulled out and spun Tiera around. As soon as she was facing him, he reached down, grabbed both of her legs, and hoisted her up.

With her legs now placed around his waist, he stepped closer to the shower wall while placing her back against it. Tiera threw her arms around his neck and bit down on the corner of her lip as she gradually slid down his pole. When their pelvises met, she slowly began to wind her hips in a circular motion using the leverage from her back being against the wall. Both Kaleb and Tiera were spent and caught in the moment, each trying desperately to bust the nut that they had been holding onto for weeks. The hot temperature of the water gradually began to change and before long, they were getting rained on by a luke warm faucet. Kaleb and Tiera both knew that in no time, it could be completely cold. Not wanting to ruin their moment, they grinded on each other harder and faster.

"Ahhh, shit...don't stop. Please don't stop!" Tiera cried out as she felt her orgasm building.

Kaleb obliged and continued to hit her spot over and over again, feeling himself about to cum as well.

Their lips met and they kissed each other like there was no tomorrow. They were not only hungry to feel the wonderful sensation they were aiming for, but they'd missed each other's presence terribly while they were apart. Moments later, Tiera threw her head back and rode the wave as an orgasm took over. Every nerve in her body came alive. With each thrust that Kaleb delivered, Tiera's body shook and shuttered. She struggled to hold on to his neck because her arms instantly felt weak. Her pussy muscles involuntarily pulsated rapidly around Kaleb's dick, letting him know that she was exactly where he wanted her to be.

Forcing her legs open wider, Kaleb raised her up and slammed her body down against his over and over again, taking her over the edge. The sound of Tiera's cries of both pleasure and pain echoed throughout the bathroom. She opened her mouth to beg Kaleb to stop, but nothing came out but moans. Just when she thought that she couldn't take anymore, she felt the familiar throbbing and knew that Kaleb was about to cum as well. Squeezing her pussy muscles as tightly as she could, she gripped his thickness, while she pulled him closer and ran her tongue across his ear. That was

Kaleb's spot, and she knew that between her licks and tightening up, he was bound to let loose. Seconds later, he did just that. With one final slam into her body, he howled and shot his load deep inside her.

Now feeling weak, Kaleb bent his knees and took a seat on the shower floor with Tiera still straddling him. He could barely move and was out of breath, but it was the best feeling in the world.

"Boy, get yo' behind up." Tiera leaned in and kissed him gently on the lips. "You act like you dying in here."

"Shit," Kaleb moaned. "Don't you ever leave me that long again. I damn near had a heart attack."

Tiera cracked up laughing. "Stop exaggerating. It was only three weeks." She kissed him again, before she placed both feet on the shower floor and stood up. This allowed Kaleb's now soft penis to slide from its hideout. "You act like I've been gone for months."

"It damn sure felt like it," he told her, grabbing her extended hand and standing up as well.

"Boy hush!" was all Tiera said in response to his silliness.

With the water cooling off even more, they both hurried to wash up, before they retreated to the bedroom.

♥♥♥♥♥

Inside his car, Kaleb maneuvered through the city headed to his destination, which was a little over thirty minutes away. As he merged onto the highway, visions of his shower rendezvous with Tiera clouded his mind. His dick jumped in his pants at the thought of going a few more rounds when he returned home. He had waited for some of her good loving for weeks and wanted to make sure that he got his fill because they never knew when she would be called away again. Kaleb was going to take advantage of all of her time while he could. Just the mere thought of Tiera made him smile. She had truly been a breath of fresh air. They had been dating for a little over a year and he looked forward to seeing where things would go. He wasn't sure if he was head over heels in love with her just yet, but did care for her a lot and when it came to Kaleb, that was a big deal.

Tiera Johnson, known to those closest to her by Te-Te, was the second woman to ever bring those kinds of feelings out of Kaleb. After his stupidity caused him to lose the only female, besides his mother, that he'd ever loved, he played the field. The only time he dealt with chicks from then on out was just for some pussy and nothing more. There were no feelings involved, no late night conversations, and definitely no spending the night. Kaleb called when he was in the mood and if they didn't answer, he moved to the next contact in his phone; it was their loss. If they did answer, he got what he wanted and moved on about his business after he was done busting his nut. It wasn't like he lied to any of them because they knew exactly what the situation was when they signed up.

Most of the women were cool with their positions, while others thought that after they've fucked him good a few times, things would change. Those were the ones that Kaleb had to completely cut off because they started to catch feelings. Popping up at places he frequented, calling his phone all times of the night, and threatening to cause bodily harm to whichever other female they caught him with was definitely a no-no in his book. It had gotten so bad that he stopped meeting new chicks and stuck with his old ones because he was tired of dealing with the crazies. That was around the time when he ran into Tiera. God must have known exactly what Kaleb needed because he sent her.

They met one weekend last year. Both were at a club that was hosting a birthday big bash for one of the up and coming rappers from Atlanta. Although Kaleb didn't club much, he tried to get out every once in a while just to kick back. On those rare occasions that he did, he always made sure that he had a section in VIP, because not only was it more relaxing, but less crowded. That night Kaleb and Desmond were being led to their designated VIP section, but were surprised to find that there were already a group of women sitting there. Confused, Kaleb asked the bouncer to go get the club manager to see what was going on, and why it was that he was standing on the outside of a section that he'd paid for. For a minute, Kaleb thought that maybe he was at the wrong section and wanted to make sure before he started to assume the worst. After looking over his list, the manager found that they had mistakenly double booked that particular VIP section.

While Kaleb and the manager spoke about him getting a refund, Tiera came over to see what the commotion was about. Upon hearing about the error, she offered half of the space to Kaleb and Desmond, since she was only there with a few of her girls, and it was only the two of them. Not wanting to leave after driving all the way there, Kaleb accepted and offered to give Tiera half of the money that he had just been refunded, but she declined. For the remainder of the night, they partied and danced together, while ordering bottles upon bottles of champagne and different kinds of liquor. When it came time to pay for the tab, Kaleb attempted to pay for it, but Tiera told him that it wasn't necessary and that she had it. That piqued his interest because he started to wonder who the beautiful woman was who hadn't batted an eye when she handed the waitress her card to pay the almost six thousand dollar balance. Before they parted ways, Kaleb asked for her number, which she gave him, and promised to call her within the next few days.

Tiera turned out to be something totally different than Kaleb was used to. She wasn't like the other chicks he'd dealt with that only wanted to be with him because of who he was and what they thought he could do for them. Although Kaleb wasn't an ugly dude, he knew that having money made him even more desirable to woman. Tiera not only came from money, but made her own as well. She was a model who worked for one of the largest clothing chains in the world, so what Kaleb brought to the table wasn't a big deal to her. Intrigued by the female who seemed to have it all on her own, Kaleb did something that he hadn't done in a while; he asked her out on a date. After that, things moved pretty quickly and they became inseparable.

"Hello," Kaleb answered his ringing phone.

"What did I do to deserve a man so sweet?" Tiera sang sweetly into the receiver. Even though he couldn't see her, he knew that she was smiling.

"What I do?" he asked, pretending as if he didn't know what she was talking about.

"I saw the luggage you bought me!" she squealed, referring to the new four-piece Louis Vuitton suitcases that he'd purchased her while she has been gone.

"Why yo' snooping ass was in my closet?" he asked laughing.

"Boy, shut up! I was looking for a shirt to wear," Tiera told him, rolling her eyes. "Ain't nobody snooping through your stuff."

"Yeah, I hear you, Inspector Gadget." Tiera giggled

at his silliness.

"Whatever crazy. I just wanted to thank you."

"You're welcome. You know I got you."

"You know I got you," she mocked him. "No, for real, I love them and even though I'm not trying to leave you for a while, I can't wait until I'm able to use them."

"No worries. It'll be sooner than you think," he assured her. "If this sale of this house I'm heading to goes through, I want to celebrate and I'm thinking about the Virgin Islands."

"Oooh baby, I would love to go back!" Tiera yelled. "Last time I was there, it was all work and no play."

"I know. I remember you telling me about it. Ya man listens," Kaleb bragged.

"That he does. It'll be just the two of us, right?"

"Yep, just me and you."

"Good. Okay, I'll let you handle your business. You just let me know as soon as you know for sure, so that I can start planning. I'll call Reeves and let him know not to book me for anything around that time, so we can relax and enjoy each other. You know I'm going to have to tell him more than once because he's going to act like he forgot. I swear that man will have me all around the freaking world," Tiera said, referring to her agent.

Kaleb laughed at her rambling. He could tell that she was excited.

"Alright, I'll keep you posted," he told her. "Oh, and Te-Te?"

"Yeah?"

"Be ready when I get back."

"I got you, baby," Tiera purred. "I'll be naked and dripping wet," she promised before she hung up.

Kaleb couldn't do nothing but smile at how lucky he was. Pushing the petal to the metal, he hurried to his destination because he was looking forward to what he had coming when he got back home.

Ten minutes later, he pulled into the driveway of the five-bedroom mini mansion that he owned along with Desmond. Kaleb glanced at the clock on his dashboard and saw that he had made it with only minutes to spare. He drove his truck up the garage closest to the home and killed his engine. When he saw that Desmond's Maserati was the only other vehicle besides his, he was glad to see that he'd beat the couple who were coming to look at the place. Kaleb leaned forward and looked out of the windshield at the property. He shook his head when he thought about just how far he and his best friend had come together.

They'd met in 2004, when they were both in middle school. Desmond and his parents had relocated and ended up moving down the street from where Kaleb lived. They immediately clicked after Kaleb stumbled upon the new boy getting jumped behind the corner store. Without thinking, he jumped in to help Desmond and from that day forward, they were two peas in a pod. Soon after, Desmond began to come over Kaleb's house all of the time. He was there so much, people in the neighborhood thought that he actually lived there. That observation turned out to be true when his mother murdered his father not even a year later, after finding him in bed with her younger sister. After she shot the both of them, she turned the gun on herself. It was the very first day of high school when Desmond came home to find his mother, father and aunt all dead in his parents' bedroom.

With Desmond not really having any other family, Kendra stepped up and took him in. Although things were already tight in her household because of her not really working, she couldn't stand to see the young man that she had grown to love put into foster care. Now with an extra mouth to feed, Kaleb came up with the idea of selling drugs. He knew that his mother was struggling to pay his brother's doctors' bills, and he wanted to help as much as he could. As soon as he pitched the idea to Desmond, he was down. Desmond would have done anything that Kaleb had asked because he figured he owed his life to his best friend.

It was the beginning of 2006 when they started to work for a local drug dealer who agreed to front them packages. They both jumped into the game head first. In 2008, Desmond was offered a full ride on a basketball scholarship, but he turned it down because he knew that Kaleb needed him more. That was the kind of person that Desmond was. He was extremely loyal to the ones that he loved, so even with Kaleb telling him to take it, he still didn't. Everything was going smoothly, for the next few years until Kendall passed away in 2009. This devastated the entire family because although they knew that he wasn't going to live a full life, they all loved him very much. By then, the boys were making money hand over fist. Since they had had a good four year run, Kaleb decided to put their money to good use and do something that he always wanted to do; and that was to flip houses. With Desmond right by his side, they did just that.

Climbing out of his Infinity truck, Kaleb fixed his jacket and slipped his keys into his pocket. As he walked up the stairs and towards the front door, he said a silent prayer that everything would work out. He and Desmond were looking to sell the fully furnished half a million dollar home, and Kaleb hoped that the guy and his fiancée wanted to buy it. They had acquired the property a few months ago and had been looking to sell since then, but they hadn't had any luck. Things like showing the house were usually done by a realtor, but since Kaleb and Desmond were both licensed, they figured they do it all and keep that portion of the money for themselves. More money meant buying more properties to Kaleb.

"Are you comfortable? Do you want me to get you a drink or something, mu'fucka?" Kaleb said when he saw that his best friend was sitting on the couch watching TV.

"Hell yeah, what you got?" Desmond grinned. He picked the remote off of the coffee table and turned off the television, before he stood up and walked over to Kaleb to give him a brotherly hug. "What's good, nigga?"

"Shit, I was just telling Te-Te that if this sale goes through, I'm taking her to the Virgin Islands."

"That's what's up." Desmond nodded his head. "Her nosy ass must have already found the luggage you bought her."

"Hell yeah, you already knew she would," Kaleb joked.

They continued to talk for a few moments, until they heard the front door open. Both men turned their heads towards the entrance. In walked a stocky dark skinned guy. He smiled when he saw the two men standing in the middle of the floor. Desmond was the first to walk over to introduce himself, followed by Kaleb, whose voice got caught in his throat when he noticed the female who entered soon after. She didn't see him, because she immediately looked down at the floor. Kaleb's eyes widened and couldn't believe who he was staring at. She had changed her hair, which had grown out a lot and was now hanging loose just past her shoulders. She was also a little thicker than she was the last time he'd seen her, but there was no doubt in his mind that it was her. He would never forget her face for as long as he lived.

"Baby, these floors are beauty-" she paused when she brought her head up and locked eyes with someone she'd thought she'd never see again.

"Excuse her fellas," the guy said, extending his hand. "I'm Deondre Godby, and this is my fiancée, Dominique McDonald.

Chapter Ten

No matter how much Kaleb tried to forget about her, he just couldn't. It had been two weeks since he ran back into Dominique, and she had been the only thing that occupied his mind since that day. Whenever he closed his eyes, she was there. It had gotten so bad that Tiera had asked if he was okay because it started to seem like he was distancing himself from her, and she didn't like it. There would be times when they were sitting right beside one another, yet Kaleb's mind was miles away. It wasn't like he was trying to; it was just that he was caught up with his own thoughts that everything around him was put on the backburner, including his girlfriend.

Kaleb thought back to the last time that he'd spoken to Dominique. She told him that she never wanted to see him again, right before she yelled out that she hated him. That day was one of the worst days of his life because he had to hear the girl he loved more than anything crying about something that he'd done. It broke his heart to know that he was the one who had caused Dominique so much pain. He tried to explain what had happed, but she wouldn't even allow him to do that. Kaleb understood that he was partly to blame for what had gone down that night, but he did not intentionally cheat on Dominique; although he didn't stop it from happening either. To make matters worse, there were pictures of what had gone down, so Kaleb knew that once Dominique caught wind of it, she would flip. That was why he had been calling her house nonstop for days afterwards, but her mother kept telling him that she wasn't available.

A few days after Dominique hung up on him, Kaleb found out that she had left her house and moved in with her grandmother and sister in McDonough. Although it was only a forty-five minute drive, it might as well had been in an entirely different state because Kaleb had no clue where to search for her. It wasn't like he had ever been to her grandmother's house before, so basically, it was like finding a needle in a big ass haystack. About a week later, Kaleb ran into Tiffany. When he asked her for the phone number to their grandmother's house, she cursed him out and tried to fight him because she knew all about what he had done. Once he was able to restrain her, she told Kaleb to stay the hell away from Dominique because he was the reason why her sister had moved away. He didn't have any luck when he approached Monique either.

Even though he could not stand Dominique's mother, he was desperate and willing to play nice in order to get back in touch with his girl. That day when Monique opened the door, she immediately pasted a devilish smirk on her face. Before Kaleb was able to say anything, she busted out laughing. Almost seconds later her, expression turned cold, and she began to explain to him just how stupid he was to have fallen in love with Dominique in the first place. She claimed that she had caught her daughter fucking one of her 'guy friends' in her bed not long ago. When she told him that, Kaleb looked at her confused because from what he knew, Dominique was a virgin. He started to tell Monique exactly that, but as soon as he started to speak, she slammed the door in his face. Kaleb stood there dumbfounded for a least a minute, wondering if there was some truth to what Monique had shared.

After that day, it didn't take long before Kaleb got so desperate that he wrote a note and asked Shanice to send it to Dominique because she obviously knew how to contact with her best friend. He waited weeks for a response, only to never get one. He asked Shanice constantly if she had given Dominique his letter, but all she said was that she had. As the days turned into weeks and the weeks turned into months, Kaleb gave up on hearing anything from Dominique. It hurt him to let her go, but he knew that he really didn't have a choice in the matter. He would think about her from time to time, but that was about it. By the time a year had rolled around, Kaleb had moved on. He was fucking with chicks here and there, but he never wanted anything with any of them. That was, until he met Tiera.

Kaleb had actually thought that maybe Tiera was the one that he was meant to settle down with; that was up until a few weeks ago. Now, he didn't know what the hell he was supposed to do. Dominique had been able to successfully elude him for more than four years. Kaleb thought that maybe she had relocated to another state, so to find out that she was still there in Georgia shocked him, and he immediately wondered where the hell she had been hiding out and what she had been up to. Once the dude introduced her as his fiancée, Kaleb was sick to his stomach. It was no secret what she had been doing after that. Although he hadn't seen Dominique in years, it still didn't sound right to hear that she was engaged to be married to someone else. She was supposed to have been his fiancée and then his wife, but one fuck up ruined that for him. Kaleb never really forgave himself for messing up things between the two of them, but he planned to make it right.

"What are you over there thinking about?" Tiera asked, lifting her head off of the pillow.

She turned on her side, slid her arm around his waist, and kiss him once on the chest.

"Nothing, just life in general," he lied.

"Ummm, okay. What do you want to do today?"

"I don't know. You wanna go to the movies later and out to eat?" he responded, looking up at the ceiling. He really didn't want to do either of the two, but knew that both were things that Tiera liked.

"Sounds good," she told him, now placing a trail of kisses down his chest and towards his stomach.

Lifting the comforter over her head, Tiera slithered under them and moved between his legs. Kaleb moaned when her tongue flickered across the head of dick, immediately waking it up. It now stood at attention and ready. Tiera gripped his penis and slowly slid it between her lips. Up and down her head went as she orally pleased her man. Kaleb's breathing quickened, and he closed his eyes to enjoy the sensation of her soft lips gliding back and forth against his manhood. Almost instantly, visions of Dominique invaded his thinking space. He tried to shake the images out of his head, but it seemed as the images were burned into his mind. While it was Tiera under the covers giving him sexual gratification, all he pictured was Dominique. This made the head he was receiving even better than it already was.

Kaleb reached down and put his hand on the back of Tiera's head, slowing her down to a speed that he desired. He wanted to fully enjoy it, and she was sucking much too fast for him. His hips lifted slightly off of the bed, as he slowly fucked her mouth. Each time he felt himself hit the back of her throat, his toes curled. Every nerve in his body had come alive. Kaleb's heartbeat raced, and his breathing was erratic. Seconds later, he brought his other hand up and put it on Tiera's head as well. This time, he changed her pace to a quicker one, bringing himself a little closer to coming. Dominique's image danced around in his head once again. The way she looked with the sheer form fitting sun dress she wore the day he'd seen her brought him over the edge. A few more pumps was all it took before he felt that all familiar tingle.

"Shit!" he grunted before he shot his load deep down Tiera's throat.

"Damn baby, either you were horny as hell or I'm getting better." She smiled after she swallowed everything in her mouth. "I ain't never made you cum that fast."

"Whew!" Kaleb exhaled, "You almost killed me."

"I try," Tiera beamed, happy with herself.

Once Kaleb came down from his high, he felt like shit. He knew that he couldn't tell Tiera the reason why he'd cum so quickly was because of the fact that he was envisioning his ex-girlfriend. That would kill her, and he would never do anything like that to her. Kaleb watched as she climbed out of the bed and made her way into the master bath to brush and gargle like she always did. Tiera was a clean freak, and even though she did whatever she could to please her man, she always made sure to clean up afterwards. Kaleb liked the fact that she kept her hygiene up, but sometimes, he just wanted to lay up after they finished having sex. That never happened though, because Tiera always had to shower afterwards, which pretty much ruined the mood.

"I'm about to go downstairs and make something to eat for breakfast. Do you have anything in mind that you may want?" Tiera asked when she emerged from the bathroom.

Kaleb sat up and looked at the woman in front of him. Her chestnut colored skin tone seemed to glow under the light shining through the open drapes and from what Kaleb could see, her body was absolutely flawless. Tiera stood at five-foot-ten and slim at one hundred and twenty-five pounds. He couldn't deny that she was definitely beautiful in every sense of the word, from her head to her feet. Tiera's naturally wavy locks, which were usually styled in some kind of big curls, hung loose and fell just above the arch of her back. Her breasts; which were nothing more than a mouth full, peeked from the bottom of the cut off white wife beater that she wore. Her waist was narrow, showing the definition of the abs she had from working out all of the time, and the dark purple low rise boy shorts she wore showcased her cute little butt that matched her toned and lean body perfectly.

"Whatever you make is fine with me, babe," Kaleb answered before she turned and started to walk away.

When Tiera looked over her shoulder and noticed that he was watching her, she poked out her butt, struck a pose, and smiled. It was then that Kaleb felt even worse than he did before. Here he was with this gorgeous woman who was willing to do anything for him, and he was stuck on the one that had left him in the past. Even after seeing him after all that time, she was still dead set on not having anything to do with him. Kaleb thought back to the day that he saw Dominique two weeks prior and shook his head at how she gave him the cold shoulder.

They were all walking around the house, while

Desmond showed them the different bedrooms and explained everything that the home had to offer. He knew that his best friend was shocked at seeing Dominique again, so he took the lead; which was something that Kaleb usually did when they were showing a home. While Desmond took the couple around the house, Kaleb brought up the rear. The entire time that they walked, all he did was watch Dominique. A few times, she turned around and caught him staring, only to look away quickly and act as if she hadn't noticed. They were on the third level of the house when she excused herself to the bathroom. Kaleb offered to show her where it was. He figured that it was the best time as any and took it as his chance to get her alone. He signaled Desmond with his eyes, who nodded, letting him know that he would keep her fiancé busy while they were gone.

"How have you been, Nikki?" Kaleb asked, once they were out of view.

"It's Dominique, and I've been great," she told him, being short.

"That's good to hear—" he started, but she cut him off.

"I thought you said that you were showing me to the bathroom. If not, I can just go back."

"It's down here and to the left," he explained, leading the way.

Dominique quickly walked ahead of him and went into the bathroom, closing the door behind her. While she was inside, Kaleb leaned against the wall. His mind was racing. He knew that he didn't have long to get her to talk to him, so he had to think quickly. Reaching into his pocket, he pulled out one of his business cards and held it in his hand. A few minutes later, Dominique opened the door and she jumped when she saw how close he was to it.

"Damn, can you back up a little bit," she told him as she put her arms out to put space in between the two of them. "I hope you weren't listening outside the door." Kaleb laughed, but when he saw she didn't, he straightened up.

"I hope you guys like the house," he told her, even though he hated to think of her and the dude as a couple.

"It's nice."

Kaleb stepped in front of Dominique and blocked

her path.

"Look, I know that you probably still hate me, but I swear, I'm sorry for the way things went down. I've missed you so much, Nikki."

Dominique seemed to be unfazed by his declaration. She rolled her eyes up in her head before she said, "Get out of my way, Kaleb. My fiancé is waiting for me."

Hearing her actually say the word 'fiancé' stung a little, but Kaleb didn't let that deter him. He had a mission to complete and he was going to do it. He reached out and handed her his card and told her to call him if she wanted to talk. It was a long shot, but Kaleb was willing to take that chance. After she took it, he moved out of her way and allowed her to pass. Again, he watched her as she walked away. By the time they both caught up with Desmond and her dude, they were almost ending the tour. Kaleb felt good knowing that she at least took his card. That meant that all hope wasn't gone. Maybe she had missed him just as much as he missed her.

When they all made it back to the living room, the men began to talk about prices and things that were *included. This lasted for a few minutes. While they talked, Dominique busied herself by going to visit the kitchen once more. Even though Kaleb's mind was on Dominique, he was still hopeful in making the sale on the house. To know that her dude was showing interest had him feeling good, until he heard him say that his son would love the large backyard.*

"Oh, I didn't know you had kids," Kaleb couldn't help to say.

"Yeah, my fiancée and I have a son named DJ," he responded with a smile.

It was then that it seemed like all of the wind had been sucked out of Kaleb's lungs. He instantly got lightheaded and had to grab ahold of the wall to prevent himself from falling. That information was something that he wasn't prepared to hear. He didn't know that there was a child involved. That made things a lot more complicated. It changed the game a little for him because it wasn't just that he had to take Dominique away from a guy that she happened to be engaged to. No, it was a lot messier. This was not only her fiancé, but the father of her child.

Soon after Kaleb came to grips with that, he

~ 169 ~

realized that Dominique had broken her own vow. Unless she had been married prior to then, she hadn't kept her promise to remain a virgin until she was married. Thoughts of what Monique had told him years ago replayed in his head, and he started to wonder if she was one from the very beginning. Just that quick, Kaleb went from surprised to feeling defeated to just plain old angry. He was angry because Dominique had made it clear to him so many times that she was not going to have sex before marriage, no matter what the case was. He begged her many times to just give it up, but she always shot him down. Now it seems it as if she had no problem doing that now.

As if on cue, Dominique came out of the kitchen. When she locked eyes with Kaleb, she rolled them and walked over to where her fiancé was standing. She entwined her arm into his and whispered something in his ear, before he turned and kissed her once on the lips. Kaleb watched her hang on his arm and giggle like a silly school girl. It made him sick. He knew that she was doing the shit on purpose to piss him off, and he hated that it was working. Soon after, Kaleb heard the words that he loved to hear and that was that they wanted to put a bid in for the house. What should have been a happy occasion was actually a depressing one. Kaleb realized that although he was selling the house and making a damn good profit, he was putting the love of his life in it with her soon-to-be husband and their child.

After seeing the so-called happy couple out, Desmond turned to him with apologetic eyes. "I'm sorry man."

"It's cool," Kaleb told him, turning to walk into the kitchen.

His throat was dry and he needed something to drink. He reached into the refrigerator to grab a bottle of water before he twisted off the top and took a long swig. When he was satisfied, he closed the fridge door and sat his water on the island. His eyes landed on a card sitting only inches away. It was one of his business cards. Kaleb picked it up and turned it around to find the words, 'Go to hell', on the back. He realized that that was the card that he'd given to Dominique. He felt rejected and came to grips with the fact that if he didn't know how she felt about him before, he definitely knew then. Tossing the card in the trash,

Kaleb went back into the living room to say his farewell to Desmond.

Turns out, they really were interested in buying the house because only a few days later, they received an offer from a realtor who was working for them. Desmond and Kaleb accepted the offer and the ball started rolling on getting ready to sell. When Kaleb got word that the house was having its inspection, he made sure that he was in attendance. He was hoping that Dominique would show up and he could get a chance to talk to her again. When he arrived, he was disappointed to find out that their realtor had showed up instead. Kaleb left the house that day with mixed feelings. He was upset that he hadn't gotten a chance to see Dominique, but was glad to make the potential sell. Now he was stuck and waiting, while he waited for the sell to go through.

"Breakfast is ready, baby!" Tiera yelled from the bottom of the stairs.

"Alright! I'll be down in a minute," he told her.

Kaleb tossed the covers off of him and shuffled into the bathroom to handle his personal hygiene. When he was finished, he put on a pair of boxers and t-shirt and headed down the stairs. In the kitchen, he saw that his plate was already made and sitting in front of where he normally sat. Tiera was bent over in the fridge looking for the orange juice and as Kaleb went over to take his seat, he paused and popped her on the ass as he passed. She laughed and shoved him in the back before walking over and filling his glass up the rim with the orange juice that she now had in her hand. When she was done, she leaned down and kissed him gently on the lips.

"I love you," she told him with a bright smile, before taking her seat across from him.

"I love you too," Kaleb replied with regret.

It wasn't that he didn't love Tiera because he loved her a lot. It was just that he wasn't sure if he loved her the way that she needed to. Before a few weeks ago, he believed he did, but now that Dominique was back in the picture, he wasn't too sure. The love that Tiera wanted and needed from Kaleb was something that he felt for someone else at that moment. Dominique still had his heart, and Kaleb knew that. He just hoped that when everything was all said and done that Tiera wouldn't be too hurt behind it. Kaleb thought about breaking things off with her, but he didn't want to take the chance of ruining what he had chasing behind someone he wasn't sure wanted him in the first place. If it happened that Dominique decided to stay with her dude, Kaleb knew that he would always have Tiera. It was selfish as hell of him to think like that, but he couldn't' help it.

While eating his breakfast, he mentally prepared himself for the battle he had ahead of him. He'd let Dominique slip between his fingers once before, and he wasn't going to let it happen again. Kaleb didn't know how long he had before she and her dude made their union official, so he knew that he had to think fast. Sitting at home stressing about what he was going to do wasn't going to cut it. He had to take action. Kaleb would be damned if the love of his life was going to marry another man, all while he sat on the sidelines and allowed it to happen. Silently, he made a promise to himself that as long as there was breath in his body, he was going to get his woman. Dominique was his, and Kaleb was staking his claim.

As Kaleb spaced out and stared into the air lost in his own thoughts, Tiera was thinking as well. She wasn't sure what was going on with her boyfriend lately, but she was going to get to the bottom of it. He was acting different, and it all started a few weeks ago when he came from showing that house. At first, she thought his change had something to do with something going wrong at the showing, but once Kaleb told her that the couple was interested in buying, she figured it was something else. Tiera wasn't sure, but her womanly instincts were telling her that a woman was involved. In the entire year that they'd been together, she had never suspected Kaleb of doing anything, so if it was a woman, she had to be special. With her eyes focused on her boyfriend from across the table, Tiera pushed those thoughts in the back of her mind. Even though she felt that her gut was telling her a storm was brewing, she hoped that it was just a false call.

Chapter Eleven

66 **A** re you coming or not? It ain't like you be doing shit up there anyways, but sitting in the damn house watching TV like an old ass lady. I ain't seen you in weeks. You ain't even tried to bring my nephew up here to see his auntie, bitch," NiChia said with an attitude. "Don't let me find out that Dre done turned yo' ass into a hermit."

"Shut the hell up Peanut, with yo' retarded ass!" Dominique laughed at how silly her sister was. "What's going on tonight anyway?"

"It's the grand opening of this club called *Forever*. It's not only ladies free all night, but free drinks for us as well. You know I'm cheap as hell, but that ain't the only reason I wanna go. I know that bitch gone be hittin', so I wanna be there," NiChia explained, "You know that I don't fuck with these hoes down here like that, so the only way I'll go is if you're with me. So, will you just bring yo' ass up here?" Dominique exhaled loudly. "Please Nikki, I don't never ask you for shit and you know it. You can come up and get cha party on with yo' sister. If not, I'm gone tell daddy."

Dominique laughed. "What daddy gone do to me?"

"Whip yo' ass when he finds out that you've been neglecting me."

"Girl bye! Ain't nobody been neglecting yo' ass." Dominique thought for a second. "I'm going to have to find a baby sitter."

"Ha, I already got that shit covered. Grandma said that she'd watch DJ. You don't ever bring him up here and she says that she misses her grandson." NiChia was laying it on thick and she knew it. "Look, I know you all Hollywood now since ya man done made it bigtime, but I figured you wouldn't be too busy to spend time with ya blood."

"Hush Peanut, with your overly dramatic ass!" Dominique yelled. NiChia was always doing too much. "I'm going to find something to wear, pack up, and I'll call you when I'm on my way," Dominique told her, mentally thinking about her outfit options. She hadn't gone out in a while and was now looking forward to it.

"Cool," NiChia giggled. She knew that her guilt trip would work on Dominique, who hated to disappoint her. "And bitch, I'm not overly dramatic. You just boring as hell."

"Boring? You reaching with that one and Peanut please, you're the most dramatic person that I know. Yo' ass is *always* doing too damn much!" Dominique laughed loudly. "You get on my damn nerves sometimes."

"Fuck you, Nikki." NiChia couldn't help but laugh herself because her sister was right. "Don't get mad at me because I have one hell of a personality. You just jealous."

"Whatever heffa. Anyways, I think I'm going to call Nicy and see if she wants to come too. We could do a girls' night," Though Dominique said it out loud, it was merely a thought.

"No the fuck you ain't!" NiChia yelled. Her happy mood was now ruined. "You talking about me? Nicy's funky ass is the *definition* of dramatic. That hoe is always exaggerating about everything and over the top as hell," she pointed out. "Plus, don't nobody want to be around her fake prissy ass. Bitch swear up and down that she the shit! Plus, that's yo' friend Nikki. You know I don't fuck with that bitch like that."

"Why though, Peanut? You are always saying that you don't like her, but you can never give me a reason why," Dominique said, moving the phone from one ear to the other. "I may be wrong, but Nicy ain't never done anything to you. Or has she done something that I don't know about because if so, please tell me?"

NiChia snorted, "See what I'm saying? That's one of the reasons why I don't like the hoe because you always taking up for her. I swear, you don't think that that girl does no wrong. I'm telling you Nikki, that hoe is sneaky. Always has been and always will be."

"Here you go. How you know she sneaky if you're never around her?"

"I ain't gotta be around to know the hoe is a snake. Tell me this, why hasn't she let you or anyone else meet her baby daddy?"

"I don't know-" Dominique started but was cut off.

"It's because it's somebody that we know. I swear, that's the only thing that makes sense!" NiChia yelled, getting pumped. "She's fucking someone that we all know, and she's keeping it a secret. For all you know, she could be fucking Dre."

"Ok now NiChia, you taking this shit too far now," Dominique warned, calling her sister by her real name. She only did that when she was serious or pissed and right then, she was both. "Dre ain't got shit to do with this. I know you don't like either one of them, but saying shit like that ain't gone fly."

"Damn, I'm sorry, alright? I'm just fucking around," NiChia apologized, "All I'm saying is that not knowing who he is means that he could be anybody."

Dominique listened to her sister's logic and couldn't help but feel that maybe she had a point. Of course, she didn't believe that her best friend was messing with her fiancé, but why would she hide her baby daddy so much if it was someone that no one knew? Even if he was some other chick's man, what did that have to do with her? She was her best friend no matter what. Dominique wasn't even sure if her parents had met the unknown guy, which made it even weirder.

Tired of speaking about it, Dominique sighed and said, "I don't know, but that ain't my business either."

She paused for a second before she continued. "Even after all that, all I'm saying is that it sucks that I can't kick it with both of y'all at once, and it's because you don't like her."

"Girl bye, you know damn well she don't like me either."

"Yeah, but only because she knows that you have a problem with her."

"Whatever, Nikki. If it's that damn important to you, go ahead and invite the bitch. Just don't expect me to play nice. That hoe got one time to say some slick shit and when she does, I'm drag her ass. Just call me when you're on your way," NiChia said before she hung up the phone.

Dominique couldn't do anything but shake her head. She knew that NiChia had an attitude, but also knew that she would get over it as soon as she saw her and DJ. They had gotten extremely close since after she moved in with her grandmother, which was next to impossible before with the way that Monique kept them apart. Back then, the girls did almost everything together before she left for college, and many times that included being with Shanice. Dominique knew how much her sister didn't like her best friend, but that didn't stop her from getting them all together every once in a while. Each time that happened, Shanice would say something that would piss NiChia off, and they would end up arguing to the point that they almost fought. It never escalated past that because Dominique would always keep them apart. She would never say it to Shanice, but she knew without a doubt that if they had actually fought, NiChia would definitely win.

"What you in here doing?" Deondre asked when he walked into the bedroom with DJ cradled in his arms.

"I'm looking for something to wear," Dominique said from inside their walk-in closet.

"Going somewhere special?"

"Not really. Peanut called and asked me to go to this party with her tonight. Grandma said she'd watch DJ, so I'm going to ride on up there," Dominique explained, stepping out of the closet with a handful of clothed hangers in her hands. "What do you have planned tonight?"

Deondre watched his fiancée as she laid a few pieces of clothing on top of the bed before she disappeared once again into the closet.

"Nothing. I'm probably going to just sit in the house and watch the game," he lied.

Unbeknownst to Dominique, Deondre was glad that she was leaving for the night. He'd already made plans to hook up with Shanice. It had been a few weeks since he'd saw his daughter and he missed her. When Deondre first told Shanice a few days ago that he would be by, he wasn't sure if that was actually the truth. Although she was still hot about him staying out all night with someone else, she calmed down quickly when he told her that he was thinking about stopping by. Deondre knew that leaving out of the house and staying gone for hours would lead to a fight between him and Dominique, and he didn't want to chance it. They had just gotten back on track, and he wanted them to stay that way. The fact that she would be gone for the rest of the night made it easier for him to do the same; he just had to make sure that he answered the phone.

Deondre stood on the opposite end of the room and watched as Dominique walked back and forth from the closet to the bed.

"I'm going to take DJ downstairs for a snack and leave you up here to do your thing," Deondre said as he turned to leave the room.

"Thank you, baby. You're a lifesaver."

Dominique signaled her blinker and merged slowly into the next lane. She sped up trying to cut her hour drive time down as much as she possibly could without getting pulled over. A quick glance in the rearview mirror brought a smile to her face. DJ was out like a light, even though they hadn't been in the car for more than ten minutes. The SpongeBob episode that was playing on the televisions mounted in the headrest was watching him, instead of the other way around. Dominique decided to listen to the radio and make her drive a much more bearable one. She really wasn't a fan of driving and jumped in the passenger seat whenever she could. Since Deondre took her almost everywhere she needed to go, she didn't have to get behind the wheel much, so this drive was going to be hard for her.

After scanning and looking for something good to listen to, Dominique stopped on a popular classic R&B station. It was on commercial, but she knew that within the next few minutes, something would come on. Almost immediately, one of her favorite songs from back when she was younger came on.

There's always that one person
That will always have your heart.
You never see it coming,
Cause you're blinded from the start.
Know that you're that one for me
It's clear for everyone to see.
Ooh baby...ooh, you will always be my boo.

Dominique turned up the volume just as Alicia Keys made her presence known. She began to bob her head and rock her shoulders from side to side to the beat. Ever so often, she would snap her fingers. Dominique laughed because she pictured that she looked just like her father when he used to dance with her at the family functions when she was a little girl. Jessie couldn't sing a lick, but would dance his ass off. Whenever Franny would put on an old song, he would jump up and drag Dominique to the middle of the floor and spin her around as if she were a princess. Even though

Dominique missed those days so much, she missed her father even more. She hadn't spoken to him in a few days and was looking forward to his weekly call. Jessie was down to his last year in jail, and he was looking forward to coming home.

Do you remember girl
I was the one who gave you your first kiss.
Cause I remember girl
I was the one who said put your lips like this.

As the lyrics from the song came to life, thoughts of the past continued to play like old movies in Dominique's mind. She shook her head when she realized who she was thinking about once again. Silently, she scolded herself because she had made a promise that he would no longer take up space in her mind. That was easier said than done because at that moment, he was all she could focus on. The time they shared together back then was such a special part in her life and no matter how much she tried to deny it, he'd made her happy, for at least a little while.

Yes, I remember boy,
Cause after we kissed I could only think about your
lips.
Yes, I remember boy,
The moment I knew you were the one I could spend my
life with.
Even before all the fame and people,
Screaming your name,
I was there, and you were my baby.

"It started when we were younger, you were mine, my boo," Dominique sang out loud. "Now another brother's taken over, but it's still in your eyes, my boo. Even though we used to argue, it's alright. I know we haven't seen each other in a while, but you will always be my boo."

Dominique's eyes watered when she realized just how strongly she was singing the lyrics. One would have thought that the person she was singing to was right in front of her, instead of somewhere else doing who knows what. Dominique changed the channel and decided to listen to one of her audio books instead. She needed to clear her mind and stop thinking so much about him. What they had was done and over, so she needed to let it go. Unfortunately for her, the soft voice of the narrator did nothing because he was still all she could think about.

It had been more than two weeks since Dominique had run into Kaleb and no matter how much she tried, she just couldn't seem to get him off her mind. Seeing him after all that time brought back feelings that she thought she left back home four years ago. She knew that she should have hated him, but the feelings that she was experience were quite the opposite. As soon as their eyes landed on one another, her heart skipped a beat. She couldn't believe that it was him staring back at her with the same shocked face that she wore. At first, Dominique thought that maybe the guy was someone who bore a strong resemblance to Kaleb, but when she turned and saw Desmond, there was no doubt in her mind that it was him. Gone was the cutie with the boyish good looks that she had grown to love all of those years ago. He was replaced with a much more sophisticated and handsome grown man.

Kaleb was fine, to say the least. At five-feet-eleven, and about one hundred and eighty pounds, he was much more athletic and built than she remembered. Kaleb was nice and muscular; not as big as Deondre, but sexy never the less. The lined up goatee that framed his jaw line gave him a very distinguished appearance. He still had those full lips that she used to love to kiss, and while she looked at him, those thoughts where the first thing that came to her mind. If Dominique were to be candid, she would say that Kaleb looked like money. When he realized that it was her, all she saw were his perfectly straight teeth that were a bright shade of white. The smile he wore on his face was one that couldn't go unnoticed. This made her happy for a minute, before she realized how bad it ended for them years prior. Kaleb had broken her heart and there he stood, grinning and shit like everything was cool. Although Dominique was secretly glad to see him, she was determined to wipe that smile right off of his face.

Just like she expected, he attempted to get some alone time with her, calling himself walking her to bathroom that he knew she could find without any help. When he slipped her his card, everything in Dominique's body wanted to keep it and call him later, but her brain told her that it was a bad idea. Not only was she engaged to be married to Deondre, but she wasn't going to allow Kaleb back into her life after he had broken her heart. He was the reason why she had to move away from home and be away from her brothers and sisters. While Dominique was happy to get away from her mother, the bond that she used to share with her sister, Tiffany, had been broken.

After she moved in with her grandmother, Dominique called the house daily, only to be hung up on by Monique. No matter how much she called, her mother wouldn't allow her to speak to her sister, it didn't matter how much she begged. This went on for a few weeks until one day, Dominique called and the number had been changed. She'd sent Shanice to speak to Tiffany but by then, she didn't want anything to do with her sister, who in her mind had abandoned her. All of that was Kaleb's fault, so if he thought that he was going to just slide back into her life, he had another thing coming. Once she coldly shot him down, she walked out of the house with her head held high. It felt good to let him know that she had moved on, even though that wasn't completely the case.

When she made it home later that day, Dominique

did a bit of digging on the internet because although Kaleb claimed to own the property, she figured that he was merely a real estate agent. He had lied to her in the past, so Dominique thought that nothing had changed. What she found pleasantly surprised her, to say the least. She discovered that Kaleb wasn't lying, and he actually did own that property and many more like it. He didn't just look like money, he had money and plenty of it. This surprised Dominique because when she left Atlanta, he was working the corners as a dealer. It was something he'd gotten into to help his mother pay for the medical care of his little brother. While his mother had insurance, it didn't cover all of the medications that Kendall had to take, so there was much more out of pocket money than she expected.

A few years had passed, and now Kaleb was buying and flipping million dollar estates as if it were nothing. Dominique thought back to when they were younger. Kaleb used to always say that he wanted to own a bunch of houses. His main dream was to help people like his mother, single parents who worked day in and day out, but were just making ends meet. For people like that, Kaleb wanted to have a few apartment buildings that would cater to the low income families. He would accept Section 8, as well as work with families to ensure that they had a roof over their heads. Dominique smiled when she thought about how Kaleb's face would light up whenever he would speak about his goals. It made her happy to know that he'd stop selling drugs and chased after his dreams instead. She couldn't help but think about how her life would have been if they would have stayed together.

As quickly as the thought popped into her head, Dominique brushed it off. She didn't want to think about things like that because it was the past, and she knew that she had to keep it there, even though it was hard as hell to do. The truth of the matter was Dominique still had feelings for Kaleb. Even after all those years, they had never changed. She had been lying to herself from the very beginning and didn't realize it until the very moment that she laid eyes on him again. Until that very day, just the thought of him still made her heart skip a beat like he did in their teenage years. She loved Kaleb then, and she loved him now, very much so. Dominique couldn't explain it even if she tried, nor did she want to. She knew that to someone else it wouldn't make sense because it barely made any to her.

She began to question why in the world she had to run into Kaleb in the first place. To make matters worse, it was the very day that Deondre had asked for her hand in marriage.

They were lying in bed when Deondre rolled over with a smile on his face. When she asked what he was grinning for, he told her that he had some exciting news to share with her. Deondre went on to explain that he had gotten an 'unofficial' welcome from the coach of the New Orleans Saints, who had been following Deondre since his first year playing football. Dominique couldn't contain herself as she jumped up out of bed, screaming about how she was so happy for him. She ran into her son's room to wake him up so that he could be a part of the great news that his father had just shared, and by the time she came back into the master room, Deondre was on his knee in the middle of the floor. In his hand, he held a small velvet box.

"I've wanted to do this for the last few weeks and now that everything is lined up, I finally can," he told her, staring her directly in the eye. "I've never loved

someone as much as I love you. It's crazy to think about how this beautiful bond started off as a friendship but grew into something so much more amazing. I'm extremely grateful to have you in my life, Nikki. You may not believe it but you've made me the man that I am today, and I owe this all to you because without your push, I would have never gone for it. For that, I will forever be in your debt. You've given me a healthy, beautiful baby boy that I absolutely adore." Tears slowly started to roll down Dominique's face as she realized what he was about to do.

"We have so many memories together, and I want to continue creating memories with you for the rest of our lives." Deondre opened the box and revealed a beautiful five carat princess cut diamond ring, before he looked her directly in the eyes. "Dominique McDonald, will you make me the happiest man on Earth and accept this proposal to become my wife?"

Dominique's face was now covered with tears. She couldn't believe that Deondre was actually asking her to marry him. Placing their son down on the floor, she smiled and wiped her face with the back of her hand.

"Yes! Yes, I would love to be your wife!" she

screamed as Deondre slid the ring onto her finger.

Right after she accepted his proposal, Deondre informed Dominique that he'd made an appointment for them to look at a house in Fayetteville. He explained that he had gotten a rather large sum of money from the Saint's coach and wanted to make sure that they had a nice home to live in before they tied the knot. Dominique was on cloud nine as she thought about everything that was about to happen. At that moment in time, she was the happiest woman in the world. Together, they dropped DJ off at Deondre's mother's house and headed to see the property. Dominique was not only ecstatic about getting married, but she couldn't wait to see the house. All that excitement instantly melted away like hot butter when she laid eyes on Kaleb.

From that moment on, Dominique begun to doubt her entire relationship that she had with her now fiancé. She coudln't deny the fact that she loved Deondre very much. It was just that she didn't love him in the way that she loved Kaleb. As hard as it was for her to admit that he was a filler, she knew that that was exactly what he was. Deondre was someone that she used in an attempted to get over her first true love. That's why it was so easy for her to sleep with him. There was nothing special about it and she knew that now. Her life was all a big lie that she just happened to be content with. It was all good up until two weeks ago. Now, Dominique was struggling with herself, as she tried to figure out how to get back on track.

As she continued to drive, she started to think about fate and destiny. She wondered if those two things were actually things that happened. Dominique realized that her running into Kaleb on the very day that Deondre proposed couldn't have been a coincidence. Was God trying to show her that Kaleb may have been her soulmate, or was the devil busy trying to throw a monkey wrench in her happily ever after?

Chapter Twelve

"I know you not gone sit over there all night with an attitude because if that was the case, I could have stayed my ass at home," Deondre snapped.

He was growing tired of the silent treatment that Shanice was giving him. Although he had only been there for around thirty minutes, it was much too long to just sit there staring at the television watching one of those corny ass reality shows. With London in bed before he even showed up, he wondered why the hell Shanice was so pressed to see him, if all she was going to do was sit there quiet. When she didn't reply, he sat there for about ten more minutes, until his anger started to get the best of him. Deondre stood up from the couch and grabbed his jacket.

"Fuck this shit. You can sit here all mad if you want to. I'm getting the fuck outta here. I got better shit to do!" he yelled as he made his way to the door.

"Why are you leaving?" Shanice whined, looking up at him.

Deondre stopped and turned around. "Come on man. I ain't got time for you and your fucking games, Nicy." He shook his head. "You wanna sit cha ass over there with the salty face for the last half hour, but when I get up to leave, you wanna talk? Fuck that."

When Deondre turned around to walk away again, Shanice jumped up from the couch and rushed over to him. "You ain't going nowhere."

She tugged on the back of his shirt and pulled him back in the direction of the couch. Slowly, he turned around and allowed her to guide him back to where he had been sitting. When he was in front of the couch, Shanice gently pushed him backwards so that he would be forced to sit down. While looking at him lustfully, she grabbed the band of her leggings and started to slide them down her thighs. When they were at her knees, she turned slightly and pushed them the rest of the way. As she did this, Deondre licked his lips as he stared at her pump cheeks that spilled out of the bikini cut panties that she wore. Although Shanice got on his nerves sometimes, he couldn't deny that she was sexy as hell.

He continued to watch her as she lifted her arms and pulled the t-shirt she was wearing over her head, before she tossed it onto the chair a few feet away. Shanice turned to Deondre and looked down at him with a slight grin. She was happy as hell that he'd actually come over because at first, she didn't believe he would. That was until Dominique called and asked her to go out. Shanice knew that with Dominique going to McDonough to her grandmother's house, Deondre would be able to stay the night with her, so she made up an excuse about feeling under the weather. Even if Deondre wouldn't have come, Shanice still would have declined the invite because she couldn't stand Dominique's ghetto ass sister, NiChia. Every time she came around, it was always some shit, and Shanice just didn't want to deal with it.

"You're something else, you know that," Deondre spoke, breaking Shanice's train of thought.

She looked down at him and innocently asked, "Why? What did I do?"

"You always complaining about me never spending

time with you and London, but when I get here you give me the silent treatment. Then when I call you on your shit and decide to leave, you chase me down and try to fix everything by fucking me."

"Oh, so you don't want me to fuck you?" Shanice asked with her eyebrows raised. She wasn't going to comment on anything else that he had said because she didn't want to fight him at that moment. She had some important news to share with him and didn't want to risk him leaving before she could tell him.

Deondre smirked. "Nah, I wanna fuck you," he told her, reaching up and grabbing her by her hips.

"How about we try something different?" Shanice spoke up when he attempted to lie her down on her back.

She was tired of the boring ass missionary position that he was always trying to put her in. Fucking on her back was something that she never liked doing. It was hard for Shanice to cum when she was lying on the bottom with someone humping you like crazy, but Deondre made sure that that's the position that they ended up in. It didn't matter what Shanice tried to do, he would always lay her on her back. She could be sucking his dick and attempt to ride him in a reverse cowgirl, but he'd spin her around and lay her down. It was like he was afraid of giving her total control of sex. Maybe had Deondre allowed her to ride him every once in a while, she could actually have a real orgasm, instead of faking them so much.

"Girl, stop playing," was all Deondre said, before he laid her back and slid her panties down her legs.

Shanice looked up at him when he stood up to remove his clothes. She wasn't looking forward to having sex with him, but knew that if she wanted him to stay, she was going to have to suck it up and let it happen. Now naked, Deondre leaned down and kissed her once on the lips. He gave her no foreplay, as he spread her legs and slid his penis inside her. *Thank God I'm always wet and ready,* Shanice thought to herself, thinking about the fact that he didn't even try to make sure that she was in the mood before he entered her. Deondre began to pump his hips rapidly. Shanice rocked back and forth against the couch, letting out a moan here and there to egg him on. *If I didn't love this nigga, I swear I wouldn't even deal with this bullshit.* While Deondre thought he was handling his business,

Shanice was lying there thinking about how she was going to tell him the news that she had been keeping quiet for the last few weeks. She didn't know how he was going to take it and figured she'd tell him soon after he got his nut.

The smacking sound of Shanice juices could be heard over the sound of the television. Deondre took her being as wet as she was as a form of letting him know that he was doing his job in the bedroom, but that wasn't the case. Shanice wasn't dripping wet from sex, it was because she loved him so much and loved having him near her. Unlike Dominique, Shanice had had other sexual partners before Deondre, plenty of them. So while Dominique thought that Deondre knew what he was doing in between the sheets, Shanice knew better. Deondre couldn't fuck to save his life, and it was women like Shanice who'd made him think otherwise.

He thought he was 'king ding-a-ling', but in reality, he wasn't working with much. This was a shocker to Shanice, who just knew with as big as he was, he would be packing at least eight or nine inches. It fucked her up when she removed his pants and saw that he was working with the dick of a prepubescent child. Still, she hopped on it because she had a point to prove and that was she could fuck anyone she wanted. It didn't bother her that she drugged him to do it, just that the fact that it was done.

"Ahhh, fuck!" Deondre moaned.

Shanice rolled her eyes, before she followed him lead. "Mmmm, yeah. Get this pussy, Dre."

Moments later, when he sped up, she knew that it was only a matter of time before he came, so she rocked her hips and met his pace. Deondre grabbed her waist in an attempt to stop her, but Shanice continued to do her thing. She was trying to get it over with, so that she could tell him what was on her mind. Not even a minute later, Deondre was yelling out that he was coming. Being the trooper that Shanice was, she began to shake and shutter right along with him, making him believe that she was as well. To make it even more believable, she clenched her pussy muscles over and over again, just to give the pulsating feeling that a female has when she's actually having an orgasm. When Deondre sat up and leaned against the back arm of the couch, Shanice got up and went upstairs. She knew he thought that she was going to clean up, but in all actuality, she was going up there to finish what he couldn't.

Inside the bathroom, Shanice opened up the cabinet under the sink and reached all the way to the back. When her hand brushed against a velvet bag, she grabbed it. Gripping the drawstring that kept her friend secured, Shanice untied it and removed a chocolate colored dildo and a small vibrator. She turned on water in the sink to not only drown out the sound, but to make Deondre think she was washing up if he came upstairs. Shanice pushed the suction cup at the base of the dildo up against the wall in her favorite place, over by the toilet. When it was secured, she turned around and spread her now cum dripping pussy lips, while slowly allowing the flexible silicon dick to penetrate her. Shanice moaned as the thick, ten-inch sex toy slid inside her, filling her tight juicy hole to capacity. She threw her head back and thought to herself, *this is what dick is supposed to feel like.* It was too bad that Deondre wasn't working with anything like that or he'd be the perfect package.

Once the toy was all the way in, Shanice grabbed ahold of the counter and started to move back and forth. The penis glided in and out with each movement, forcing Shanice to bite down on her bottom lip. She hadn't been fucked so good since the last time they had a date. It was a shame that the only way she could get off was to fuck a plastic dick that she had stuck to the wall in her bathroom. If she didn't love Deondre so much, she would find her someone to fuck on the side. Truthfully, she should have done that anyway, he was. Instead, Shanice remained faithful to a man who was not only taken by none other than her best friend, but was fucking other people as well, and this was something that Shanice knew for a fact, at least one person anyway. Even though that pissed her off, it wasn't enough to make her stray because Shanice knew that if Deondre thought she was fucking around on him, he would cut her off. She'd rather continue to fuck her plastic man, while praying he didn't find out about that because that was a form of cheating to Deondre as well.

"Mmmm, yes," Shanice moaned, picking up the pace. When she felt herself getting closer to coming, she lifted her leg and placed it on the toilet seat, before she turned on the vibrator and placed it against her now fully exposed clit. "Ahhhh, shit."

With her right hand gripping the counter and her left hand holding on to the vibrator, Shanice pushed herself against the dildo rapidly until she came. Hot sticky liquid oozed out on her hand, as she continued to move her hips, this time much slower. When she couldn't take anymore, she placed the vibrator on the counter and slid off of the now glossy sex toy that was still secured against the wall. Shanice took a seat on the top of the closed toilet lid to compose herself before she cleaned everything up, put it all back, and retreated back downstairs. When she rounded the corner to the living room, she saw that Deondre was still sitting in the same spot as he was when she left. His head was leaned back and when she got closer and saw his eyes closed, she realized that he was sleep.

"Dre, get up," she whispered while slipping on her t-shirt and underwear. "Dre?"

"Huh?" he responded sleepily. His eyes opened slightly and he stared at her, wondering why in the hell she was waking him up.

"Get up. I need to talk to you."

"Tell a nigga later. I'm sleep girl," Deondre snapped, closing his eyes again. He was getting irritated with her because had just gotten his nut, and all he was ready to do was go to sleep. He wondered why she was tired, after he had just beat it up.

Shanice sighed, "It's important." She knew she was pushing her luck, but she had to tell him something and that moment was the perfect time.

"Damn, Nicy!' Deondre yelled, opening his eyes and flinging his arms to his side. He sat up straight on the couch and stared at her annoyed. "What...what the hell is so important that you couldn't just tell me in the fucking morning?"

With a lump in her throat, Shanice looked him dead in the eye and whispered, "I'm pregnant."

♥ ♥ ♥ ♥ ♥

The usual forty-five minute drive to his house took closer to twenty. Deondre sped all the way there, only stopping once he arrived at home. Pulling into this driveway, he jumped out of his car and slammed the door shut. His phone continued to ring in his pocket while he walked up the stairs to him home, but he ignored it like he'd been doing for the last twenty minutes. He knew it wasn't anyone but Shanice anyway, and he didn't feel like talking to her stupid ass. Once inside the house, he tossed his keys on the table in the foyer and kicked off his shoes across the room. Dominique wasn't home to flip out on him about making a mess, so he took advantage of it.

Deondre's first stop was the liquor cabinet that they kept in the corner of the dining room because he definitely needed a drink. He didn't even bother to grab a glass, opting to drink directly from the bottle of *Jack Daniels*, which was the first thing he laid eyes on. At that moment, what kind of drink it was didn't matter, he just needed to ease his mind. Deondre plopped down on the couch and turned the bottle up. He shook his head and licked his lips as the brown liquid glided down his throat. *What the hell have I done?* He wasn't prepared to hear Shanice tell him that she was pregnant for the second time. Although he was shocked, he really shouldn't have been. It wasn't like they had been using protection. He knew she was also not on the pill, so really, what did either of them expect? He understood that they were both at fault for her pregnancy, but he still found a way to place the blame on Shanice because in his mind, she should have known better.

Deondre's logic was that Shanice knew that he was in a relationship with her best friend, so he wondered why on Earth she would continue to sleep with him. He was a man and that was what men did, but she was supposed to be Dominique's 'bestie', as they called themselves. Having sex with one another's men and ex's were off limits, yet she didn't seem to have a problem with it. Shanice was already doing Dominique dirty by having her claim their child as her God-daughter, and now she planned to bring yet another kid into the mix. It was fucked up. There were all kinds of emotions running through Deondre's mind at that moment. He was mad because Shanice should have never allowed herself to get pregnant in the first place. *She should have gotten on the fucking pill, the shot, or something,* he rationalized.

Deondre was beginning to feel a series of emotions. One was fear. He hated to think about what would happen if Dominique was to ever find out about the two of them. *Would she leave me and take my son away, or would she stay and try to work it out?* These were questions that he'd asked himself, even though he never wanted to know the answers to them. Dominique was his world, and he couldn't imagine his life without her, even if it was because of something stupid that he'd done. Deondre knew that he was fucked up, but wasn't going to go down without a fight. Shanice was just going to have to keep that baby a secret as well. She knew what she was getting into from the beginning, so now just because there were two children involved, she couldn't switch up. No, she had to continue to play her role.

Deondre scolded himself for continuing to mess with her in the first place. The night that they fucked the first time, he should have told Dominique then and things would have been a lot smoother now, well, at least he thought they would have been. Even after she called and told him that she was pregnant, he should have gone ahead and confessed, instead of putting himself into even more messy situation. That would have been the most logical thing to do, but since Deondre was thinking with his little head, he allowed her to pull him into her deceitful game. He couldn't understand how a girl, who claimed to love her best friend so much, could go behind her back and fuck her man, even if it was a mistake the first time, like she claimed. The crazy thing was that Deondre still didn't know just how he ended up in her bed in the first place. The last thing he remembered was drinking, before he woke up naked beside her.

Although he couldn't prove it, he swore that Shanice had done something to do with them sleeping together that night. She was sneaky like that and that was why from that moment, he always kept his eyes on her. Even with that being said, Deondre just couldn't stay away. It was something about Shanice that kept him coming back, and it wasn't just because she had some good ass pussy. No, it was something else. Something he just couldn't figure out for the life of him. Deondre talked all that big shit when Shanice pissed him off, but he couldn't imagine his life without her either. He didn't love her the way that he loved Dominique, but he loved her and cared about her wellbeing. At first, he used to say that it was only because she was the mother of his daughter, but after a while, he knew that it was much more than that.

Even with all of the love that he had for her, Shanice wasn't and would never be the 'wifey' type for

Deondre. She wasn't someone that you would take home to your mother or hell, even your father. Not only was she hot in the ass, but she had an aura about her that made you think that she thought she was better than you. It may have been from the way she was raised because she had always been spoiled rotten, but even then, her parents never acted like that. No matter who you were, they welcomed you with opened arms and never judged you, well that was at least how they acted when Deondre was around. Whether fronting or not, Shanice was the total opposite.

She looked her nose down on almost everybody because she thought that they were beneath her. Deondre wasn't sure, but maybe that was why he was so drawn to her. She was nothing like what he was used to. The bright colored weaves she usually wore were always extremely long and hung all the way down past her butt. Shanice also wore makeup all of the time, and even though she was a pretty girl without it, you would never know because she always had it caked on. Then it was that ugly ass septum nose ring that she thought was so cute. Even that became sexy to him after a while, although he would never tell her that. Shanice thought she was the baddest thing walking and even though she was a pretty girl, with a sexy ass shape, she had nothing else going for her. All she wanted to do was look pretty, talk like she was big shit, and spend money, and that was something that Deondre grew to accept.

It pissed Shanice off to know that 'plain Jane', the named that she always called Dominique behind her back, had stolen his heart. Deondre was no fool. He always knew that Shanice had a crush on him when they were younger, he just never looked at her like that before. She stayed in his face during every family function and no matter where he went, she was there smiling and shit. Deondre really started to notice when she began to wear tighter jeans, shorter skirts, and lower cut shirts. Even still, he ignored her as much as he could, until he saw that she was slacking up with the flirting. That was cool with Deondre though because he was trying hard not to hurt her feelings. What Shanice didn't realize back then was that she was just like all of the other girls that he never paid attention to, always flashing and wanting to be seen.

As he took another swig from the bottle, he thought about what he was going to do about his new situation.

His phone vibrated in his pocket. Removing it, Deondre glanced at the caller ID and saw that it was, in fact, Shanice calling him once again. After she hung up, he went to her contact and blocked her number. He knew that Shanice would be mad when she figured out what he had done, but he didn't give a damn. He had to get his mind right. He was only going to keep her there for a few days. He had just grown tired of her calling back to back. Not only that but he knew that he needed a few days away from her, so that he could get his mind right.

With the bottle in his hand, he stood up from the couch and made his way across the room, before taking the stairs two at a time. Inside his room, he removed his clothes and left the heap in the middle of the floor. Deondre climbed into the bed and laid down on the pillow. His head was starting to spin from the effects of the alcohol, and it only intensified his headache. He was stressed out. Although he was sure that Shanice wasn't going to say anything to Dominique, he knew that this situation could not really be a lifelong secret. She was already nagging him about not spending time with his daughter like he did with DJ. His family didn't even know anything about London at all and that was something that Shanice didn't like. While she knew she was only the side chick, her child was not. Sooner or later, his infidelities were bound to come out, and Deondre wasn't sure what he was going to do then. At that moment, he just wanted close his eyes. He'd figure out the next step when he woke up the next morning. When his phone vibrated alerting him of a text message, he shook his head because he thought that somehow Shanice had found a way to get through.

Baby Luv: Goodnight Dre. I love you.

When Deondre saw that it was Dominique, he smiled before he immediately started to feel like shit. There she was, out clubbing with her sister and thinking about him, while he was at home trying to figure out how he was going to hide yet another baby that he'd had on her. Deondre wasn't sure of exactly what he was going to do, but he knew that he needed to get his shit together. The number one thing on the list was to stop fucking her best friend. Deondre knew that he couldn't honestly marry Dominique while he was still dealing with Shanice, so he had to find a way to break it off. That was a task in itself. His heart hurt just thinking about letting her go. There was no doubt that he was selfish. He wanted his cake and ice cream too.

Shanice had already proven herself to be a snake, so he had to choose his battle wisely. There was no telling what she could do once she realized that she had nothing left to loose and that was what scared Deondre. Shanice held secrets of his that he never wanted anyone to know. Even though she swore to never tell a soul, he couldn't be too sure. Women do crazy shit when you fuck them over and that was exactly what she would feel he did. Shanice couldn't even be loyal to the person who she called her best friend, so what would make him any better? Deondre had to think of a plan and soon, before his entire world blew up in his face and he lost everything.

Chapter Thirteen

"It's packed as hell in here!" Dominique yelled over the music. "It seems like everybody in Georgia is in attendance," she joked, looking around at the mass of people all around her.

She had just finished texting Dre and wished like hell that her 'goodnight' really meant it for herself because she really didn't want to be there. She and NiChia were at the bar that NiChia had told her about and it was packed. It was just the two of them because Shanice claimed that she didn't feel well and couldn't tag along. Dominique knew that she was more than likely full of shit because when she spoken to her earlier, she didn't say anything about feeling sick. Her fake ass illness was probably triggered by her no-good ass baby daddy coming over. Dominique started to drive over to her house and do a pop-up, just to see what the hell she was doing, but changed her mind at the last minute. She had promised her sister that they were going to kick it, and she wasn't going to mess that up chasing after her best friend, who didn't want to be bothered anyway.

"I know! I told you this bitch was gone be jumping!" NiChia responded, raising her voice as well. "Let's go get a drink!"

Together, they made their way through the crowded club and over to the bar. As they walked closely together, Dominique could feel a pair of hands grabbing at her. She turned up her face to the ugly light skinned guy who had the audacity to grab her arm as she passed. He smiled and pulled her closer, while trying to whisper something in her ear, but she smacked his hand away. *Thirsty ass muthafucka!* she thought to herself, while rolling her eyes. NiChia noticed what had gone down and laughed at her sister, whose face was still twisted in an evil scowl. It took them a few more minutes and a couple more 'excuse me's' to make it to the bar, and when they got there, they saw that even that was overcrowded.

"I don't see why you like shit like this," Dominique complained. "It's too many people in here to do anything."

"I know. I didn't think it would this crowded," NiChia agreed. "It's mostly these stankin' booty ass bitches. Remember I told you that it's free tonight for ladies, and they get to drink for free. You know these hoes love free."

"Heffa hush! Yo' ass act like that wasn't the main reason you wanted to come," Dominique put her on blast. "You gotta lotta nerve." She laughed.

"Fuck you, Nikki, with yo' stankin' ass," NiChia rebutted. "Just for that, I ain't ordering you a drink."

"So bitch, you act like you buying it. They free anyway."

NiChia rolled her eyes before she turned around and tried her best to flag down the bartender. It seemed like he went everywhere other than where they were standing, and she immediately got irritated because she knew that he more than likely didn't see her short behind over the crowd of much taller people.

"If they let one mo' muthafucka in here, the Fire Marshall gone fuck around and shut this bitch down."

"I don't think that would be a bad thing,"
Dominique mumbled.

They had only been there for less than a half hour
and she was already ready to go. It was too many people
in one place, and she couldn't see herself having fun at
all, especially since there was only enough room to
stand. With the heels she was wearing, she couldn't
picture having to be on her feet for the rest of the night,
but by the looks of things, that's exactly what was going
to happen. While NiChia continued to try to get the
bartender's attention, Dominique turned and looked
around the club. Other than being extremely packed, it
was a pretty nice place to party.

There were two levels to the club. In the middle of
the first floor sat a very large oval shaped bar that was
surrounded by lights. Two others were on each opposite
end of the room, yet they were only about half of the
size of the main one. There were large round lanterns
hanging from the vaulted ceiling, which gave the place
just enough lighting to set the mood. Marble pillars
with beams were placed sporadically around the
building hosted a few strobe lights that rotated all
around the floor. Even though there were around

twenty or so long suede couches aligning the walls and around the dance floor, there were so many people that there were literally no available spaces left. It was so bad that there were chicks propped up on their friend's laps, just to have somewhere to sit down.

What really caught Dominique's attention was the VIP section that was on the second floor away from the normal crowd. From where she was standing, she could tell that there were eight of them because the only thing she could see was the balcony. Each appeared to be extremely spacious. They had to be because each two took up an entire wall of the rectangular shaped building. Even though there were people up there, it was a lot less crowded than it was on the first floor. Dominique smacked her lips because that was where she wanted to be.

"We need to be up there!" Dominique yelled to NiChia, who was still struggling to get the bartender's attention.

"You do." She heard over her shoulder. "You can come up to my section if you like."

Dominique blew a bunch of air out of her mouth before she turned around, ready to tell whoever it was in her ear that she was not interested.

"I'm good. I'd rather..." she stopped when she realized who the mystery man was.

"How you doing, Nikki?" Kaleb said with a sly smile.

He and Desmond had been sitting upstairs in their section when he caught a glimpse of her standing in the middle of the floor. When she started to walk away, he feared that she might have been leaving, so he damn near broke his neck to catch her. Desmond came along to see who the sexy ass female she was with was. He had never seen her before and wanted to feel her out.

"It's Dominique, and I'm doing alright." She smirked. It was hard to pretend that she wasn't happy to see him because she was. "What are you doing here?"

"What's up, Nikki!" Desmond interrupted as he stood behind Kaleb.

"Hey Des, how have you been?" Dominique asked, reaching her hand out to shake his hand. She jumped when he pulled her towards him and wrapped his arms around her.

"Don't try to play me like that girl. Yo' nigga ain't

here, you can show yo' boy some love." Desmond laughed, squeezing her tight.

When Desmond let Dominique go, she turned around and was met with a strange look from NiChia. The look clearly asked who the hell dude was, and why did he have his hands on her.

"Peanut, this is Des...I mean Desmond," Dominique started her introduction. "Desmond, this is my sister, Peanut."

"How you doing, Peanut," Desmond spoke while staring NiChia up and down. The jean shorts she wore showed off her thick thighs, and her small breast spilled out of the top of her low-cut shirt. There was no doubt that he liked what he saw.

"I'm good, but you can call me NiChia," she replied, giving Dominique the side eye for passing on her childhood name to the handsome stranger.

"Damn, it's like that?" Desmond asked with his face twisted up. He didn't know ole' girl, but she was starting to rub him the wrong way already. If there was one thing he couldn't stand, that was a stuck up bitch. She was fine, but having a fucked up attitude would make her unattractive as hell.

"Nah, it's not like that. It's just that's my childhood name, and I'm not really too fond of that now," she replied, glancing at Dominique once again.

"A'ight, cool. I understand." Desmond felt better knowing that she just wasn't stuck up like he thought.

"I'm Kaleb, by the way," Kaleb spoke up when he noticed that he wasn't going to be introduced.

"Kaleb?" *Why does that name sound so familiar?* NiChia thought to herself. "Kaleb...wait, you're not *thee* Kaleb, are you?"

"Yeah, I guess. It depends on which Kaleb you're referring to," he said with a chuckle.

"Humph, I've been wanting to kick yo' ass for the longest." NiChai told honestly.

Kaleb thought that she was joking, but when he noticed the evil look that she was throwing his way, he knew that she wasn't. Not wanting to mess things up even before they started, he glanced towards Dominique, cleared his throat, and said, "I have a section up there. You both can come up if you want." He paused and looked down at Dominique. "It's a lot less crowded up there," he added.

Dominique thought about it for a minute before she

responded, "Nah, we good."

"Are you sure?" Kaleb asked in a smooth tone but inside, he was panicking. When Dominique nodded, he turned his attention towards NiChia. He hoped that she would be more obliged to come up and sit with them. "Tell your sister that she can come up. I promise I won't bother her," he said in a pleading tone.

"We're going to have to pass homie," NiChia told him with an evil eye. Although she wanted to fuck Kaleb up, she was still dying to go. Of course she wouldn't tell him that. "It's about time for us to leave anyway. It was nice meeting you Desmond." She smiled.

Kaleb watched in defeat as NiChia grabbed Dominique's hand and together, they made their way to the exit. Right before they disappeared through the crowd, Kaleb had an idea. If Dominique thought she was going to get away from him that easy, she was sadly mistaken.

"Hello?" Dominique answered the phone groggily.

"Good afternoon beautiful." She heard on the other

end.

It took a minute before she realized who it was. This brought a bright smile to her face.

"Who is this?" she asked, just to mess with him.

"It's Kaleb, is this a bad time?"

Dominique stretched her arms high above her head and glanced towards the alarm clock. When she saw that it was a little after one in the afternoon, she rolled over to see if DJ was still asleep. The side of the bed that he'd slept on was empty, which let her know that either NiChia or her grandmother had already come in to get him.

"Nah, it's cool. I needed to get up anyway," she told him, sitting up in the bed. "Wait, how in the hell did you get my number?"

Kaleb chuckled lightly before he replied, "I have my ways."

"Is that right? Well, what can I help you with Mr. King?"

"Mr. King huh? Alright, I'll let you have that.

Anyways, I know you have your thing going with your man and all, and I don't want to disrupt that," he lied. Kaleb wanted nothing more than to break up their union, so that he could slip in and take over what was his in the first place. "I guess I just really want to talk."

"About what?" Dominique questioned.

She stood up and walked over to the window and looked out. From where she stood, she could see NiChia in the front yard chasing DJ around. He stumbled trying to get away, while she pretended as if she couldn't catch him. Dominique could tell that they were both having a blast, and she was glad that she decided to go ahead and visit because it had been a while.

"Just talk. I know that things ended pretty badly between us, and I just want to clear the air." When Dominique didn't answer right away, he did something that he hadn't done since they were teenagers. He begged. "Please, Nikki. All I want is an hour of your time. If afterwards you decide that you don't want to hear from me again, I promise I'll leave you alone."

"Kaleb," Dominique exhaled.

As much as she wanted to play the hard role, she knew that she did really want to see him. Part of her just wanted to be in his presence, while the other part of her wanted to at least hear what he had to say for himself. She never got any closure after their breakup because she stopped talking to him. She had made Shanice swear that she would never bring it up again because the details were something that she didn't think she could stomach. Now that Dominique was grown, she was prepared to hear him out, no matter how painful it may have seemed.

"Okay, where you do want me to meet you?" When Kaleb heard her say that, he got happy as hell because he knew that it was his chance.

A half hour later, Dominique was pulling up the destination. When she saw Kaleb standing outside with a goofy grin painted on his face, she couldn't help but smile. He was just so handsome. She killed her engine, reached over, and grabbed her bag, before she stepped out of the car and walked over to where he stood.

"What made you pick this place?" she asked, when she was standing in front of him.

"I like their Italian Ices, and I think you will too," Kaleb responded. "Plus, there's a park across the street, and I figured we could sit on the bench and talk."

Dominique shrugged her shoulders and followed behind Kaleb as they both entered the place called *Rita's Italian Ice.* It took a few minutes for Dominique to figure out what she wanted, so she allowed Kaleb to pick for her, and she went with the Green Apple Ice. Once they got their order, together they walked across the street and took a seat on one of the nearby benches. The two sat in silence for a few minutes, each caught up with their own thoughts. When five more minutes passed, Dominique started to wonder if Kaleb was going to speak up. She was giving him a chance to talk to her, yet he wasn't doing that. Meanwhile, Kaleb sat there soaking up the fact that she had actually agreed to come, so he was happy just to be around her. As he sat there scooping up his Italian Ice, he was also stuck trying to figure out exactly where he should start. There was so much that he wanted to tell her, but he knew that he didn't have much time. Dominique's presence also made him nervous, and he didn't want to say something to run her off because he wasn't sure if he would get another chance to speak to her.

"You never told me how you got my number." Dominique said, turning to look at him.

Kaleb laughed nervously, "I know someone who works at Sprint. I gave them your name, and told them to look you up. He couldn't find you, so I asked a few other people. Turns out, you got Verizon."

"Boy!" She laughed as she pushed him. "You are so damn crazy."

Although Dominique didn't say it out loud, she was flattered to know that he went through all that to find her number. After sharing a laugh, they went back to the quiet. This last for a few more minutes before she couldn't take it anymore.

"Kaleb," Dominique started, finally breaking the silence once again, "didn't you say that you wanted to talk?"

"Yeah...I did."

"You haven't said a word since we've been sitting here. What's the problem?"

Kaleb cleared his throat. "I want to first start off by saying thank you for meeting me. I also want to say that I'm extremely sorry for everything that went down back then. I never wanted to hurt you—" he began.

"It's okay. I'm not even tripping over that anymore," Dominique lied, cutting him off. She refused to let him know that she was still hurting behind it years later. "That was the past, and I've moved on, Kaleb. You should too."

"I know that you've moved on," he responded, hating to admit that she actually had. "It's just that I can't. I have to tell you this, so please...please just let me finish." When Dominique nodded her head to let him know that she would, Kaleb continued. "The day that we had that argument in my room, I was out of line and I knew it. I never meant for what I said to come out that way. I guess it just slipped. Then when you walked out, I figured that we both just needed time to calm down, and that is why I didn't chase after you, even though I really wanted to. You and I both know that you probably would have tried to fight me, as mad as you were." Kaleb chuckled, lightening the mood.

"Hell yeah." Dominique laughed along with him.

"Anyway, I ended up calling you that night to try to apologize, but Tiffany picked up and told me that you weren't there. I figured you told her to tell me that, and you were still mad."

"No, that wasn't the case," Dominique explained, "I actually wasn't there. I had spent the night at my grandmother's that night. "I didn't see Tiffany until the next day, but some crazy shit happened, and I guess it slipped her mind," she said, not mentioning the fact that the 'crazy shit' was her mother swinging on her grandmother and her beating her mother's ass behind it.

"Well, that explains it," Kaleb realized. "All this time I thought that you were still mad at me. I figured I would just see you at the party and explain everything then. Truthfully, that's the only reason why I went in the first place. I wanted to talk to you."

"Humph," was all that Dominique could come up with. Looking back on things, she wished that she would have made it to the party. Maybe things would have turned out differently.

"Of course, you know I ended up going to the party. Crazy thing is that shit didn't turn out the way that I thought they would. I planned to talk to you and we'd go back to the way things were. Instead, shit got fucked up."

Dominique thought about just how fucked up things had turned and soon after, her stomach started to feel queasy. With her appetite now gone, she dropped the plastic spoon into her cup and sat back on the bench. She really wanted to tell Kaleb not to talk about what had happened that night, but remembered that she'd promise to let him finish his story, so that was what she was going to let him do. All of Dominique's attention was now on Kaleb. She watched as he took a deep breath and started to tell her about the chain of events that led to him breaking her heart.

"When Des and I got there that night, I went around asking everybody if they had seen you, but no one had. I figured you were running late, so I decided to sit on the couch in the living room and wait for you to show up. I had been sitting there for close to two hours when Shanice came over and sat beside me. I asked her if you had come with her, and she told me that she hadn't heard from you that day, but that you were probably on your way." Dominique looked over at Kaleb curiously. When he noticed she stared at her the same way before, he asked her, "What's wrong?"

"Nothing, I was just thinking about the fact that I'd called Shanice earlier that day, so she already knew that I wasn't coming to the party. I even told her to tell you that I would call you later once the party was over,"

Dominique explained, still wondering why her best friend hadn't given him her message like she claimed she had.

"I swear she never told me that. If she had, I would have taken my ass home right then. I told you I was only there because I wanted to talk to you."

"Wow, that's crazy."

"I know." He didn't really speak on it, but finding out that information had Kaleb mad as hell. Had Shanice told him that Dominique wasn't coming, things could have, no scratch that, would have turned out much differently. "Anyway, we talked for a few more minutes about school and other bullshit, before she disappeared and came back with a drink for the two of us. I took the drink, she left, and I drunk it while continuing to wait on you to show up. Maybe an half hour later, I realized that you weren't coming. I figured your mother more than likely said no and because we hadn't talked the day before, you didn't get a chance to let me know. By then, I was ready to go. I got up to go use the bathroom because I was going to let Des know that I was leaving afterwards. As I walked up the stairs, I started to get dizzy. By the time I got to the top of the stairs, somehow, I slipped right outside of the bathroom and fell on the floor." Kaleb shook his head.

"Now, I know that I'm not the type to drink a person under the table, but I know for a fact that I'm not a lightweight drinker either. There is no way in hell that one drink, no matter what kind of liquor it was, would put me on my ass like that." Without saying anything, Dominique agreed with Kaleb. In the two years that she had known him, he had had his share of alcoholic drinks and never had she seen him so messed up that he'd fallen. "Well, out of nowhere, I heard somebody ask me if I was okay. When I looked up to see who it was, I saw a girl standing there. Before I even got a chance to say anything, she walked over to where I was lying, helped me up, and together, we stumbled into the bathroom."

"So, you didn't know who this chick was?" Dominique asked because she remembered that Kaleb and the girl that he had cheated with had been talking prior to the act.

"No, I didn't," he answered. Dominique gave him a look that said that she thought that he was lying. "I swear to God, Nikki. I didn't know who that chick was,"

Kaleb proclaimed.

"Alright, go head," she urged him to continue.

"Well, I was so confused by what was going on that when she sat me down on the closed toilet seat, all I could do was sit there. I guess I was trying to get my bearings together. I never got the chance to though because she walked over toward me and started to unbutton my jeans. I remember smacking her hands away a few times, but she just kept at it. Before I knew it, she had taken my dick out and put it in her mouth." Kaleb looked up at Dominique with regret written all over his face. "I was so drowsy and fucked up, I could barely keep my eyes open. I swear, all I wanted to do was go to sleep. It was as if I was drugged or some shit. As she continued to do her thing, I just closed my eyes and allowed my body to drift into the rest that I so desperately wanted."

"Than what happened?" Dominique asked, even though she really didn't want to hear it.

"Honestly, I don't know. When I woke up, Des was standing over me, smacking me in the face and yelling my name." Kaleb looked up at the sky. "The next thing I remember is waking up at home. When I talked to Des, he told me that I had fucked up and everybody knew about it. I still don't really know what happened that night," he told her truthfully. "Like I told you before, I didn't even know who the fuck that girl was. I had never laid eyes on her before that day, so why in the hell would she be sucking my dick in the bathroom at a party?"

"I don't know Kaleb."

Kaleb sat his cup down by his feet and turned to Dominique. "I swear to God, I didn't intentionally cheat on you. You gotta believe me," he pleaded, taking her hands into his. When he saw the doubt on her face, he spoke again, "I know it's been years since it happened, but why would I lie now?" Dominique wiped away the tears that had fallen from her eyes with the back of her hand. She hated that he still had that effect on her. "If I could take it all back, I would. You gotta believe me when I say that I'd give up everything I have to make things right with you."

"It's too late Kaleb," Dominique whispered.

"It's never too late to start over," Kaleb rebutted. He wasn't going to let her get away that easy. "Just tell me that you forgive me and that we can move on and be friends."

Dominique nodded her head and Kaleb smiled, happy that she was at least giving him a chance. They talked a bit more about what had gone on since they'd been apart. When he told her about Kendall dying, Dominique was heartbroken. She felt so bad for Kaleb because she knew how much he loved his little brother. Tears poured down both of their faces when Kaleb explained just how it tore his mother up. Kendra lost it when her baby boy died. She was so messed up that she had to be taken away from the funeral home in an ambulance because she had literally passed out. Dominique's heart ached when she saw Kaleb in that much pain. When she pulled him in to hug him, they kissed, and even though they broke it quickly, they both felt the surge of electricity that they felt from each other's tongue. Neither of them knew it, but that was just the beginning.

Chapter Fourteen

"What you got planned to do today?" Deondre asked from the bathroom.

"I don't know. I was thinking of going shopping for a few things and getting my nails done," Dominique replied, stretching her arms high above her head. "Other than that, I ain't got shit on my agenda."

Stepping out of the bathroom, Deondre stood in the door with a towel wrapped around his waist. "What you think about getting married in the next month or so?" he questioned, catching Dominique off guard.

"What?" Although she had heard him correctly, she had to make sure of exactly what he was saying.

Deondre laughed nervously. "You know damn well you heard me girl."

"Yeah, I did. I just wanted to make sure I wasn't

tripping."

"You ain't."

Dominique looked at him strangely, before she sat up in the bed and asked, "Why do you want to get married early, all of a sudden?"

"Damn, can't I just want to get married before I leave for training camp?"

Dominique looked across the room at him. "I'm not going anywhere. So, if that's what you're worried about, you can rest easy," she assured him.

"I'm not worried. I just don't want to wait!" he snapped. "We've been together for three years already, so why shouldn't we go ahead and do it now?"

"Because I don't just want to rush and get married!" she told him, not liking the way he was now speaking to her. "I could have sworn that we both agreed that we would wait until we were able to get settled, before we planned a wedding. I was thinking it wasn't going to be until next year sometime or maybe even the year after that."

"Well, I don't want to wait that long," Deondre retorted before he turned around and made his way back into the bathroom.

Dominique looked in that direction with her head cocked to the side. *I know the fuck he didn't just walk away from me like what he said was what it was gone be.* She threw the covers off of her body and climbed out of the bed. *He got me fucked up!* Now with an attitude, she followed him into the bathroom. When she got there, he was standing at the sink with his toothbrush now in his mouth.

"I know you tripping," Dominique said, getting his attention.

Deondre looked at her through the mirror, before he nonchalantly asked, "Tripping about what?"

He knew what she was talking about, he just wanted to hear her say it. He wasn't going to speak about it, but it hurt his feelings to not have her jump at the thought of marrying him soon, even though she had no clue that he was doing it just to lock her down before the storm that he knew would come sooner or later. He also figured that it was a lot harder to leave your husband than it is to just walk away from your baby daddy. Deondre knew how Dominique felt about marriage. She always said that she only wanted to get married once because whoever her husband was, she planned to spend the rest of her life with him. She had known all about how her parents had gotten together and didn't want anything like that. The man she planned to marry was going to be someone that she loved unconditionally, and not a person who she settled for.

"Don't play with me, Dre. You know exactly what the hell I'm talking about. How the hell you gone say, *I don't want to wait that long,* and walk away like that was the end of the discussion?"

Now irritated himself, Deondre turned to face her with a scowl on his face. "First of all, I didn't walk away like shit. I asked you a question. You told me how you felt and I told you how I felt. You don't wanna get married right now, then fuck it. I ain't even gone worry about it."

"You can't be serious right now," Dominique scoffed. "How the hell you gone get mad at me because I don't want to just rush and get married, just because you decided to change your mind not even five minutes ago!"

"I didn't just change my mind. I've been thinking about it for a while. I was just asking—"

"Well, yo' black ass should have bought it up then!" Dominique cut him off. "Then you have the nerve to get pissy with me because I don't agree. This is not what I planned, and I'm not fucking doing it, so you can stay mad."

"So, that's how you feel?" If Deondre's feelings weren't already hurt, they definitely would have been at that moment. "If things don't go Nikki's way, then they don't go no way?"

Dominique raised her hand. "You can stop right there! Nah, you ain't about to do that boo." She stepped further into the bathroom. "Don't you try to twist this shit around and make this about me."

"And why not? It's you who don't want to do it right now. Who the hell else can I make it about?"

There were times like this that Deondre wished that he wouldn't have spoiled Dominique as much as he had. It was hard to talk to her because everything had to go her way, or not at all. She didn't care if you agreed or how you felt, as long as she was happy, and he was starting to get sick of it. Without even waiting for her to reply, Deondre stormed passed her and headed into their bedroom. He had to get out of there before he said something that he really didn't mean. There was enough on his plate and dealing with Dominique's spoiled ass was something that he wasn't in the mood for.

"Go ahead and leave like you always do when shit gets real. Pretend you're going to practice, out to drink with the boys, or to whichever bitch you run too when we have problems. I honestly don't give a fuck, Dre!" Dominique yelled over his shoulder. "Just don't expect me and DJ to be here when you get back. I'm leaving too. I'm tired of you running away from your problems like a little punk ass boy!"

At the speed of light, Deondre was in her face. He moved so fast that he dropped his towel and was now standing in front of her naked. His face was twisted in an angry scowl, and the veins in his neck were pulsating. Dominique had never seen him that mad before and for a brief second, she wondered if he was going to hit her. Bracing herself, she prepared to fight his ass back if need be. She wasn't going to allow anyone to put their hands on her and not get hit back. Dominique knew that she couldn't physically beat her much taller and stronger fiancé, but she was going to damn sure try. Deondre was going to think twice before he ever put his hands on her again, not that he would get another chance because once he did it once, it was over for the two of them.

"You watch your fucking mouth," he growled through clenched teeth while pointing his finger in her face. "Don't you ever in your fucking like call me a punk again. I'm a grown ass man, and you better address me as one!"

Dominique stared at him with absolutely no fear. He had her seriously fucked up. "If you don't get your mutha'fucking finger out my face, we're going to have a problem," she told him, as if she could really beat his ass.

Neither of them said anything else, as they continued to just stare at one another. Before long, Deondre turned around and walked away shaking his head. While Dominique stood there staring daggers into his back, he snatched his drawer out and grabbed something quick to throw on. He was done arguing with her ass for the day and needed to get out and get some air. Deondre figured it was best if he left because with as angry as he was, he was liable to do anything at that moment. Dominique could stay in the house by her damn self and think about what was on the line. She had a man who would give her the world, yet she chose to let her selfishness get in the way. Granted, Deondre was cheating on her, but other than that, he was the perfect gentleman; a perfect gentleman on the rise. Things were looking up for him, and he wanted nothing more than to bring Dominique along for the ride.

It had been almost a month since he had gotten drafted to the *New Orleans Saints* and soon, he would be leaving for training camp. Dominique didn't understand that he had a lot on his plate. Not only was he going to be leaving her, DJ, and his family behind, there were so many things that could go wrong. He could be injured during training camp or cut altogether. On top of that, he had the Shanice issue. Now fully dressed, Deondre walked passed Dominique, who was still standing there glaring at him. If looks could kill, he knew that he would have been buried last week. Without so much as a word, he grabbed his cell phone off of the nightstand and stormed out of the room.

"Something's going on with dude," Kaleb told Dominique. "Mark my words."

"Why do you think that?"

"Because, why else would he be in such a hurry to marry you now. You said that the both of y'all had already planned to have a long engagement, now all of a sudden he changes his mind. Something is up," Kaleb pointed out.

Dominique thought about what he was saying for a minute and couldn't help but to agree. Deondre had changed up on her out of the blue, and she wanted to find out why, especially after watching him lose his cool over the fact that she didn't share his enthusiasm. Usually, Dominique wouldn't have brought up anything that was going on with her and Deondre to Kaleb. It was disrespectful and messy as hell to talk about your relationship with someone on the outside, but she couldn't help herself because at the moment, she really needed someone to talk to.

"You may be right," she replied, still in deep thought while she reclined back her seat.

They were sitting in his car parked outside of one of

the condos he owned, waiting for a potential buyer to show up and view it. After Deondre walked out of the house, Dominique kept her promise by making sure that she and DJ would not be home whenever he decided to bring his ass back to the house. As soon as she heard the front door slam, she grabbed her overnight bag from her closet and filled it up with her belongings, before doing the same thing to DJ's things. Once she had everything packed up, she jumped in her car and headed to her grandmother's house, where she planned to stay for the next few days. She called NiChia while she was driving, but her phone went straight to voicemail. Dominique expected to see her sister once she got to their grandmother's, but Franny told her that NiChia hadn't been home since the day before. Now worried, Dominique called NiChia's phone back to back, but continued to get the same result. It wasn't until an hour later when she called Dominique back and let her know that she was alright and with a friend. Who that friend was, Dominique did not know because NiChia wouldn't share that information.

That was around the time that Kaleb called. He hadn't heard from her in a few days and wanted to check on her. Since the day at the park, they had been keeping in touch. Talking to one another had become a pattern for the two of them, with Kaleb making sure to send her a 'good morning beautiful' text daily, just to let her know that she was on his mind. Even though they hadn't done anything sexually, Dominique still felt guilty. Talking on the phone with one another was still a form of cheating, so for the last few days, she had started to keep her distance from Kaleb. That was until Deondre pulled that stunt earlier that day. When she saw his number flash across her phone, she hurried and picked it up. Although she didn't have plans to tell him, Dominique had missed talking to him. With nothing much else to do, Dominique left DJ with her grandmother, while she and Kaleb went to grab something to eat. While there, he asked if she wanted to ride along with him to show a place that he was trying to sell. Since Dominique loved to look at houses, she agreed.

"This sneaky ass heffa." Dominique jerked her seat upward and looked out the window. "I guess it's safe to say that I know who her special *friend* is now," she said. When she heard Kaleb laughing, she looked in his direction. "You knew where she was the entire time and didn't tell me?"

Still chucking, Kaleb shrugged his shoulders and said, "That ain't none of my business what those people do."

"Bullshit!" Dominique yelled, before she punched him in the arm, bringing even more laughter.

Dominique opened the car door and marched over to where the pair was standing and placed her hands on her hips. They were so caught up in their conversation that neither of them even knew that she was standing there. With her head cocked to the side, Dominique cleared her throat.

"I guess I ain't gotta ask ya what you been up to."

"Girl, what the fuck you doing here?" NiChia asked. When her eyes landed on Kaleb, who was now leaning against his car, she smirked. "Never mind, I already know."

"Uh huh bitch, don't even try it." Dominique wagged her finger in the air. While they were talking, Desmond walked away and over to where Kaleb was. "He just came to pick me up not long ago, grandma said that yo' ass ain't been home since yesterday." She turned her nose up. "I don't even wanna know what yo' lil nasty ass been doing."

"Well damn Mrs. Jordan," NiChia said, taking a step back.

Dominique looked at her like she had lost her mind." Who the hell is Mrs. Jordan?"

"My gynecologist bitch, since you so worried about my pussy." Both women burst out laughing at how silly and vulgar NiChia was.

"I swear I hate you so much!" Dominique laughed.

"No you don't hoe, you love me."

"That I do. You still get on my damn nerves though." Dominique replied still laughing.

Kaleb and Desmond walked over towards them and together, they all went into the building and to the elevators. While they rode up, the girls continued to make girl talk. NiChia told Dominique about how she and Desmond had ran into each other a few days after she introduced them in the club. They exchanged numbers and started to talk on the phone. Soon after, he invited her on a date, and they had been kicking it ever since. Dominique still couldn't believe that they had been talking for almost a month, and she didn't know a thing about it. She had to admit though, they looked good together. When the elevator stopped, the group stepped out and made their way to one of the two doors that were on that floor.

As soon as they stepped inside, Dominique's mouth dropped. She loved it! There were wall to wall windows. Since they were so high up, she could pretty much see the entire downtown Atlanta from where she stood. Dominique only imagined how good it looked at night when everything was all lit up. She broke away from the group and started to give herself her own tour. The first place she headed was to the kitchen, which turned out to be fit for a chef. There was a professional grade stove and a double oven attached to the wall. The microwave, dishwasher, and huge fridge were all stainless steel. There was even a large island, which had enough space for at least six barstools. Even the kitchen had the magnificent view.

"You like what you see?" Kaleb asked.

Dominique was now in the master. She looked in awe with how big the bedroom was. There was a king sized bed in the middle of the floor, but even with it being there, it was still more room. Attached was the master bath, which housed a jetted tub, glass shower, and two huge his and her closets. There was even a water closet, which is where the toilet was enclosed with a separate door. Although she was used in living in a nice home with Deondre, it wasn't as nice as what she was looking at. It kind of put her in the mind of the house that they were about to buy. Dominique couldn't wait to decorate it and was counting down the days until they closed.

"This condo is the shit!" she exclaimed.

"It is. I originally bought it for myself, until I came across this other one that I think fits me more. It's away from the downtown traffic that I hate so much."

"Look at you, baller," she joked, nudging him.

"Nah, I ain't a baller. I'm just an average Joe tryna make it." He smiled.

"See, that's what I love about you. You're so down to—" Dominique paused when she realized what she had just said.

"Girl, I love this place!" NiChia yelled as she walked into the room, saving her sister from futher embarrassment.

"Me too," Dominique agreed, before she grabbed

NiChia by the arm and led her out of the room.

♥ ♥ ♥ ♥ ♥

"Oh my God, what are you doing to me?" Dominique moaned.

Her head hung off the side of the bed, as Kaleb pumped in and out of her at a steady pace. She wrapped her arms tightly around his neck and pulled him closer. A low moan escaped her mouth before she bit down on her bottom lip. Kaleb sat up on his elbows and looked her in the eye. His stare was so intense, that she was forced to look away. He wasn't having it though and grabbed her face to turned her head back to face him once again. This time, she didn't look away, opting instead to match his stare. Keeping eye contact during sex was something new for Dominique. When she and Deondre were in bed, she always covered her face with her hand, while making sure that the room was extremely dark. To say that she was shy was an understatement. She didn't even allow Deondre to see her naked, and they had been together for three years. This is why it amazed her that she was buck naked having sex by the window with all of the lights on. Kaleb just had that effect on her.

It was the second day in a row that she tangled in between his sheets. After the showing of the apartment the day before, she and NiChia accompanied Kaleb and Desmond to the movies. It felt so fun to be out with them; almost too fun. Dominique started to feel bad about being out with Kaleb behind Deondre's back, so after the movie was over, she asked him to drop her off at her grandmother's. Once there, she sat with Franny and DJ for a while, before she retreated to her old room. Since she hadn't heard from Deondre since earlier that day, she picked up her phone and decided to give him a call. Even though he had acted an ass towards her, she felt obliged to call him after kicking it with Kaleb all day. The phone rang a few times, before she heard a male's voice pick up. Immediately, she knew that it was Pierre.

"Hey Pierre, can I speak to Dre?" she asked, all while she wondered why the hell Pierre was answering his phone in the first place.

"Hey, Nikki. Hold on for a minute, he's sleeping," Pierre told her. There was a small pause before

Dominique heard him say, "Dre, Nikki's on the phone. Dre," he called out again. It sounded like he was rocking him. "Nikki is on the phone."

"Man, fuck her!" Deondre barked in a sleepy tone. Dominique's mouth dropped open. *No the fuck he didn't.*

"Don't pay his ass no mind, Nikki. He's been drinking," Pierre tried to explain, but she wasn't trying to hear it.

"Don't even worry about it Pierre. When his funky ass wakes up, you tell him that I said, fuck him too," Dominique said before she hung up her phone.

She laid in the bed with tears streaming down her face. She was more angry than hurt because there she was, feeling bad about kicking it with another nigga, and Deondre was still acting like an asshole. Thoughts of what Kaleb had said earlier that day replayed in her mind. *Dre's ass is up to something. He gotta be,* she rationalized. *There was no way in hell that he would be this mad about a damn wedding, unless he was trying to get married for another reason.* Not one to worry about it too much, she picked her phone back up and dialed up Kaleb. When he told her that he would be there in thirty minutes, she let her grandmother know she was leaving back out and went to get dressed.

"Damn," Kaleb groaned, "you so fucking sexy."

He lifted up and grabbed her left breast with his hand and placed it in his mouth. Gently, he sucked on her nipple, ever so often grazing it with his teeth. Dominique arched her back to give him better access because it felt so fucking good. Before she knew it, her eyes were rolling into the back of her head. She was in heaven. Kaleb sucked on her breast for a few more minutes, before he grabbed both of her legs and placed them onto each of his shoulders. He started to go long and deep, just the way he knew she liked it. Dominique's mouth formed into an 'O' shape, and she threw her head back. Kaleb was hitting her spot, a spot that she never even knew she had. Drops of sweat fell from his face and landed on her stomach. He was working hard, and Dominique appreciated every stroke he delivered. Moments later, she started to feel that tingle, a tingle that she had never before felt before yesterday. She knew that she was almost there.

"Don't stop!" she cried out. "Don't you fucking stop."

Kaleb followed her instructions and continued to pound away at her creamy center. He was glad that she was almost there because he had been holding his nut in for the last few minutes, and couldn't wait to let it go. He pumped a few more times and when her body started to tremble, he knew that she was there. Dropping her legs, he slid his hands underneath her ass and dug into her deep. Each time his pelvis rubbed against her, Dominique moaned.

"Ahh, shit! Right there...ahhh, right there," she whined. "Baby, I'm about to cum."

Dominique's body jerked and jumped, as if she was being electrocuted. Every nerve in her body was alive, as she rode the way to her orgasmic bliss. Kaleb groaned when he felt her pussy muscles start to clamp and release his dick over and over again. He was now at the point of no return. *How the fuck is she so tight?* He gripped her hips even tighter and closed his eyes. Each time his pelvis slammed into hers, it brought him even closer to releasing his load.

"Fuuuuuuuck!" Kaleb yelled, still pumping in and out of her. With each stroke, he felt the cum drain from his dick and into the condom he wore. "Goddamn girl, you got some good pussy," he told her, once he was finished.

"Why thank you, sir, you working with something special ya damn self." Dominique laughed. When he rolled off of her and onto his back, she leaned over and kissed him once on the lips.

"You better stop, I think I got one more in me."

"Boy hush." She giggled.

Dominique laid down beside him. With a smile on her face, she scooted closer and when Kaleb felt her, he put his arm around her and snuggled up. She hated to say it, but that moment felt so right. Dominique knew that she was wrong for cheating on Deondre, but she couldn't help herself. It didn't make it any better that he was basically pushing her way because she didn't want to get married right at that moment. Pushing her deceit to the back of her mind, Dominique thought about just how different Kaleb was. Sex with him was so much more pleasurable than it was with her fiancé. Deondre was a take charge kind of guy. He always wanted to be on top and in control. They had never had sex any other way other than missionary, even though Dominique asked him to fuck her from behind. Dre shut her down quick by saying that doggy style was for gay niggas, and he wasn't about to do no gay shit.

Dominique had also never been on top before when it came to Deondre. Kaleb, on the other hand, loved to have participation. So when he asked her to ride him the night before, she had no clue what she was doing. It wasn't that she was terrible, it was just that she couldn't find her rhythm right away. This baffled Kaleb because he couldn't understand how she could have been in a relationship with her baby daddy for three years and had never rode a dick before. He didn't mind showing Dominique exactly how to do it. It was as if she was a virgin to him because there had been so many things that her dude had never done with her. This was fine with Kaleb, who planned to teach her everything he knew and mold her to fit him perfectly.

When Dominique heard a light snoring, she knew that Kaleb was sleeping. Still wrapped up in his arms, she closed her eyes as well. She wasn't sure what she was going to do, but she had to figure it out because she knew that she was playing a dangerous game.

Chapter Fifteen

"Do you know what you're drinking?" NiChia asked as she looked over the menu.

"Nope, not yet. I'm trying to wait until Nicy gets here to order," Dominique replied, looking toward the front of the restaurant. When she heard her sister exhale loudly, she glanced across the table at her. "Don't start no shit, Peanut."

NiChia never pulled her eyes away from the menu. "Do I ever?" she replied.

Dominique was about to say something in return, but when she looked up, she saw her best friend coming. Shanice strutted towards them with a look on her face like she knew she was the shit. She wore an all-black, low cut romper, which left very little to the imagination. It was so tight, you could see her coochie print, but of course, Shanice knew that. On her arm was a bright pink Michael Kors satchel that matched the thin belt around her waist and the six inch pumps she wore perfectly. Her now pink colored sew-in was parted on the side and styled with loose flowing curls that cascaded down her back. They were meeting at the Olive Garden to have lunch before going to the movies, and she walked in like some stripper looking for a tip.

NiChia looked up at her and rolled her eyes. "This bitch," she mumbled slightly above a whisper.

Dominique cut her eyes at her sister, as to tell her keep her mouth closed, before she stood up to great her friend.

"Hey boo." She smiled.

"Hey chica," Shanice sang. "What you been up to?"

"Nothing, just taking it day by day. You look cute," Dominique told her as they both took their seats. "I love your hair."

Shanice ran her fingers through her curls. "Thank you. I just came from the shop. That tramp Trina had me in there all day."

"I don't even know why you complaining because she does that every time you go." Dominique laughed.

Shanice couldn't comb hair to save her life. She was so bad at it that even at three years old, London was going to a hairdresser to get her hair braided and beaded.

"I know right," Shanice agreed. "How you doing, Peanut."

"I'm good," NiChia replied with a fake smile. "You?" Although she didn't give a damn, she asked just to pacify her sister.

NiChia couldn't stand Shanice. Not only did she think that she was a sneaky, jealous, and conniving bitch, she didn't like the fact that she always walked around with her nose in the air. For as long as NiChia could remember, Shanice always though that she was better than everyone else. Although they all grew up in the same neighborhood, she believed that since she came from a two parent household, she was more superior to the other kids. It didn't matter that NiChia and Dominique had two parents in there house as well, or at least for a while they did. The fact that her parents spoiled her and gave her everything she wanted only made her worse. Back then, anytime Dominique got something new, Shanice had to have something new as well. Whether it was a baby doll or a pair of shoes,

Shanice wanted it. It was like she was in competition with a girl that she claimed as her best friend. Dominique didn't seem to notice that she was extremely jealous of her, but NiChia saw it from day one.

Shanice ran her hand across the back of her neck and tossed her hair over her shoulder, before she said, "I've been doing alright."

For the next two hours, the ladies made small talk while they drank and ate. If you were on the outside looking in, you would have thought that they were all best friends by the way they laughed and joked. That couldn't have been further than the truth. In reality, the only person who was having a good time was Dominique, who was glad to see her sister and best friend getting along. She had no clue that both women secretly stared at the other with hate in her eyes whenever she wasn't paying attention. When it was time to pay the bill, Dominique took care of it. Since it was her who planned the girls' day, she figured that she might as well pay for it.

Full and satisfied, the trio left the restaurant. Dominique and NiChia climbed into her car, while Shanice opted to drive alone. She did this for two reasons. One, she refused to sit in the backseat. She knew that since NiChia had rode there with Dominique, that she was more than likely going to be calling shotgun. Two, she loved her new Benz. She had only had it for a little more than a week, and she was looking forward to rubbing it in Dominique's face. She knew that they were wondering if she was driving her parent's car, and she couldn't wait to pull alongside Dominique's Acura and let her know that the car was in fact hers. Her father had purchased it for her as an early present for her birthday, which was the following month.

Thirty minutes later, both cars were pulling up at the movie theater on Mt. Zion road. Shanice climbed out like she was a movie star and stood in front of her vehicle. She watched as Dominique and NiChia talked for a minute before their doors opened. Shanice couldn't do nothing but shake her head because she knew that the two jealous bitches were more than likely talking about her. She didn't mind though because she was used to being the topic of conversation.

"This is nice, bitch," Dominique said when she climbed out of the car.

"Thank you. Daddy got it for me about a week ago

for my birthday," Shanice told her, slapping her hand against the hood. She wanted to make sure that she knew that it was hers. When she saw NiChia giving her a mean mug, she decided to fuck with her a little bit. "Have you gotten you a car yet, Peanut?"

NiChia's eyes narrowed. "Yeah bitch, you been knew I had a car. Don't be trying to be funny," she snapped.

"Excuse the fuck outta me! I wasn't trying to be funny. I was just asking if you had a fucking car. You can keep the attitude," Shanice retorted, rolling her neck.

"And you can shut the fuck up!" NiChia took a step towards Shanice, but before she got close enough, Dominique grabbed her arm.

"Alright y'all, the movie is about to start," Dominique interjected, while pulling NiChia in the opposite direction.

Shanice hit her locks and followed the two sisters toward the theater. While she walked behind them, she laughed to herself at how easy it was to get NiChia upset. She was so predictable. Any little thing someone said to her could get her riled up. It was like fighting and talking shit was all she knew how to do. *Ghetto ass bitch,* she thought as she watched Dominique pulled NiChia towards her and whisper something in her ear. NiChia snatched her arm away and started to speed walk ahead of her sister. Shanice could tell she was mad, but really didn't give a fuck. If she already had an attitude, NiChia was going to be pissed by the time that she was through with her. Shanice was going to show Dominique just how bad of an idea it was to have them both together when she knew that they couldn't stand one another. It was all a part of the plan to put a wedge between the two sisters, who were way too close in Shanice's opinion.

At the ticket stand, Dominique paid for three tickets to see *The Purge.* She had seen the preview on television not long ago and was looking forward to seeing it. Since Deondre didn't like movies like that and she didn't want to see it alone, she figured that she'd see it with her girls. After stopping at the concession stand and spending damn near a hundred dollars, they grabbed their snacks and were all ready to watch the movie. The theater was slowly filling up, so they took the seats in the middle row and prepared to watch the movie.

"This shit is about to be fucking crazy," NiChia said, while placing a piece of popcorn in her mouth. She had put the slick shit that Shanice had said in the back of her mind and was ready to enjoy the movie.

"Hell yeah!" Dominique agreed as the lights lowered.

♥ ♥ ♥ ♥ ♥

"I can't even imagine what would happen if they legalized crime for twelve hours for real," Dominique said as they exited the theater. "People would be doing all kinds of shit. Niggas would be robbing, looting, and killing the entire time. It would be a fucking holiday."

"You ain't lying. You know it would be a bunch of ghetto ass black people throwing trash cans through store windows trying to get all the free shit they could," Shanice added.

"You do know that white people loot too," NiChia told her.

"That may be true," Shanice tossed her hair over her shoulder, before she continued, "but they don't do it half as much as these project ass people who ain't never had shit."

NiChia looked at her like she had lost her damn mind. "Do you have something against black people because last time I checked, yo' ass was just as black and just as ghetto."

"Come on y'all," Dominique interrupted. She already knew where this conversation was headed, and she didn't want to see it escalate. It was no secret that NiChia was still feeling some kind of way about the car comment from earlier, and she knew that it didn't take much more to set her off.

"Nah, Nikki," Shanice put her hand up, "let me tell this girl something." She hit the alarm to her car and unlocked her doors, before she opened the driver's side and placed her purse in the seat. "I may be black, but I damn sure ain't ghetto. You can say what you want, but you know not even you believe that."

"Bitch please," NiChia scoffed, "you ain't fooling nobody. You just as ghetto as the rest of us. You can walk around here like yo' shit don't stink, but I know better. You'se a fucking fraud." She was tired of playing games with Shanice and was finally about to tell her exactly how she felt. It didn't matter what Dominique said. She could be mad at her for all she cared. She'd get over it sooner or later.

"A fraud huh? How you figure?" Shanice stepped from around her car door. "Hoe, ain't nothing about me fraud." She laughed. "I'm quite possibly one of the realest bitches you've ever met."

"Let's go, Peanut." Dominique attempted to grab her sister, but she snatched away.

"Bitch please! Who the fuck done pumped yo' head up?" NiChia countered, taking a step closer in her direction. "Don't let these nigga's gas you up boo-boo because you faker than that hair on top of those nappy ass roots." She gestured towards Shanice's head. NiChia was only a few words away from knocking the shit out of out.

"That's funny. Let's be real for a minute, hoe. Not only do you wish you could afford this hair, but you wish you could be me," Shanice snarled. "I see how you always looking salty when I come around. You've been jealous of me since we were younger, with yo' broke ass. The only reason you're even here is because Dominique invited you and paid for everything. She's *always* taking care of you. Don't you get tired of mooching off your sister?" she asked, getting loud. "You twenty-one years old and ain't got shit. You live with your grandmother because nobody wants yo' ass-"

Before she was able to finish her insult, NiChia hauled off and hit her dead in the face. Shanice's head jolted backwards, and her body flew into her car door, forcing it closed. Not giving her a chance to recover, NiChia rushed over to her and proceeded to hit her with left to rights. She was tagging her opponent with every shot, while Shanice swung wildly, trying to get her off of her. When one of Shanice's hands came down and scratched NiChia on the side of the face, she grabbed a hand full of her hair and slung her over toward Dominique's car. There, she proceeded to hit her over and over again with her free hand. Dominique screamed and grabbed her sister by the back of her shirt, trying to pry her off of her best friend. By now, there was small crowd of people who were still leaving out of the theater, walking their way. The loud argument got their attention, but the brawl brought then closer. Little by little, they started to surround the fight, some even pulling out their cellphones and recording every move. Dominique tugged at NiChia's shirt with much more force when she heard someone yell out, 'Worldstar', because she refused to let her sister and best friend become one of those videos that she hated to see.

"Peanut, that's enough!" she yelled, still pulling on her shirt. It was no use because NiChia was in her zone.

"Get the fuck off my hair bitch!" Shanice screamed. "That's all you can do is pull my hair!"

As soon as she said that, NiChia let go of her hair, stepped back, and posted up. With her fist balled tightly, she bounced from side to side like a pro boxer, waiting for Shanice to make her move. NiChia knew that her sister's best friend was no match for her, even though she was almost a half a foot taller than her, so she wasn't worried. Shanice talked a bunch of shit, but couldn't back it up and now was NiChia's chance to show her that she didn't know who she was fucking with. The only reason that she had let go of Shanice's hair was because she wanted to give her a fair one. NiChia knew that she had hit Shanice with a cheap shot and didn't want to give her a chance to use that fact as a reason she had gotten her ass beat.

Shanice raised her fist up in front of her face. NiChia looked at her weak attempt to square up and laughed. Maybe if she wasn't too busy trying to be cute, she would have learned how to fight like her and Dominique had. Unfortunately for Shanice, NiChia was a natural born scrapper. She had hands like a boy, and had even given a few of them a few beat downs. She had gotten her fighting skills from a mix of her mother and Jessie. Back in the day, Nicole was a mess. NiChia had heard stories about her mother fighting almost everyone in the neighborhood. She used to beat up everybody who thought that just because she was a mere five feet, she was too little to take up for herself. These fights went on until the summer that Nicole turned seventeen. That was when she found out that she was pregnant with NiChia. After that, she slowed down and settled into being a mommy.

"Come on bitch!" Shanice yelled, putting up a front. She was scared shitless of NiChia actually running up on her again, but with so many people out there, she wasn't going to let her know it. "Wanna sneak me and shit."

NiChia smiled because she knew that Shanice had

no clue what her hands were capable of. She stepped towards her and hit her with a quick jab in the face. She followed up with a series of lefts and right, all of which connected. Shanice threw a few weak shots, but none of them had any effect on her rival, who was brushing them off as if they were nothing. The two women continued to take swings at one another while the crowd watched anxiously. When Shanice tried to throw a haymaker, NiChia dodged it and came back with a right hook that put Shanice on her ass.

"Peanut, let's go. That's enough," Dominique said once again, trying to pull her sister in her direction.

NiChia smirked down at Shanice, before she allowed her sister to guide her away. She knew that she hadn't gotten a chance to really beat Shanice's ass the way she really wanted to, but the little damage that she had done would definitely make her think twice about coming at her crazy in the future. When NiChia turned completely around to walk away, she stumbled when she felt something hit her in the back of the head. Lifting her hand to the spot where she had been struck, she gasped when she pulled it away and saw blood. *Oh no this bitch didn't.* NiChia turned around just in time to see Shanice bending down to pick up something off the ground. *Did this bitch just hit me in the fucking head with a rock?*

With the rage of an angry bull, NiChia snatched her arm away from Dominique and charged at Shanice. When she tackled her and they both fell to the ground, nothing could be heard but a bunch of "ooh's" and "ahhh's". NiChia didn't care about none of that shit, she was only concentrating on beating the hell out of her component. Shanice had fucked up and threw something at her and made her head bleed. She was going to pay, whether she knew it or not. Dominique ran over in an attempt to grab her sister again, but she was pulled back by somebody from the crowd who wanted the fight to go on. She turned around and saw that it was a dark skinned guy. His gold grill showed when he smiled because apparently, he thought it was funny.

"Get the fuck off of me!" she yelled as she swung on him, hitting him square in the jaw. When she saw a flicker of anger wash over his face, she prepared herself for a fight, but instead, he let her go.

Dominique looked at him in disgust, before she

rolled her eyes and pushed through the crowd that was now surrounding the fight completely. By the time she was able to get back to the fight, she saw NiChia on top of Shanice holding her hair with her left hand, while bring her right up to punch her in the face. There were bits and pieces of pink hair lying all over the ground. Shanice looked helpless as hell as she kicked and screamed for NiChia to get off of her. The legs of her romper were now dirty and rolled up her legs, and she was missing one of her shoes. Just as Dominique got close enough to grab NiChia once again, her sister yanked Shanice by her hair and started to drag her across the parking lot.

"No!" Dominique shouted. This must have got her sister's attention because she stopped dragging her. Dominique sighed in relief because she thought that it would be the end of the fight, but she couldn't be more wrong.

"Bitch!" NiChia yelled, throwing a punch.

The sound of bones cracking forced Dominique to look away because she knew that her best friend's nose had been broken. This didn't bother NiChia at all because she continued to hit Shanice again and again, after every few words she spoke.

"I told yo'..." *Bam* "dumb ass..." *Bam* "that I was gone beat yo' ass one day..." *Bam* "but yo' ass ain't wouldn't listen." *Bam* "Now..." *Bam* "you wanna scream and shit! Dumb hoe..." *Bam*

"Peanut!" Dominique screamed again.

She grabbed ahold of NiChia's arm and pulled her with all her might. Because she was still holding on to Shanice's hair, her head jerked a little bit and she cried out. Dominique pleaded with her sister to let go and before long, NiChia did. Once there were no more traces of Shanice's hair in her hands, Dominique drug NiChia towards her car. When they got there, she opened the door and pushed her inside, before closing it behind her. She shot evil looks at all of the spectators that were standing around. It had to be at least forty people out there now, with most of them being men. Dominique couldn't believe that not one of them had even attempted to help her break up the fight. She knew that if she'd had some help, the fight wouldn't have gone on for as long as it did.

By the time Dominique got back over to Shanice, she was off the ground and leaning on her car. Blood leaked from her nose and her left eye was partially closed. Her hair was all over her head and had pieces of gravel all through it. When she saw Dominique coming, she turned her back to her and leaned down to look in her mirror. Shanice was mad at her as well because she believed that Dominique must have wanted her to get her ass kicked. There was no way in hell that she couldn't have broken up the fight before she had and saved her the embarrassment of getting beat up like that in front of all of those people. Just thinking about the fact that the entire thing had been recorded made her sick because she knew what would happen once it was uploaded to social media. She had seen her fair share of fights on Facebook and wasn't looking forward to all the many people who were going to crack jokes about her, just like she had done to many girls before.

"Are you okay?" Dominique asked.

"Do it look like I'm okay?" Shanice barked. "I think my fucking nose is broken." She leaned down to spit, and there was nothing but blood present.

Whoop-Whoop

Dominique looked in the direction of the sound and saw the police pulling in. She cursed under her breath, because if they saw the condition that Shanice was in, there was no way that someone wasn't going to jail. Dominique hoped that her best friend wouldn't finger her sister as he attacker, choosing to just settle it between the two of them. She knew that she would have no such luck when she saw the smirk on Shanice's face, and knew that shit was about to get real.

Chapter Sixteen

Dominique paced back and forth across her living room floor. With her phone to her ear, she dialed Deondre's number, only to have it once again roll over to voicemail. After leaving him yet another urgent voicemail, she hung up and called him again. She had done this for the last two hours. After speeding all the way home from the movie theater, she was still getting the same result. She hoped that whatever Deondre was doing was important because to ignore her calls for the last hour was too much, especially when he didn't have a clue what she was calling for. It was an emergency and apparently, he was too caught up in whatever he was going to even care. Dominique exhaled with an exaggerated breath. She was irritated and antsy. She needed money, and he was the only person she knew had it.

After hanging up her phone once again, Dominique took a seat on the couch and leaned back. She still couldn't believe what had gone down just a few hours prior. When the police pulled up at the movie theater, she thought that they would ask a few questions about what happened and hoped that Shanice would either downplay the situation or accuse someone else of her assault. Neither of the two happened. Soon, two male Caucasian officers stepped out of the patrol car, one fat and one skinny. Shanice immediately fell out crying. Dominique looked at her and shook her head because she knew just what was about to go down. She stood there and watched as her best friend put on a show of a lifetime, as she cried and gave details about the fight that were not true.

Shanice claimed that they were coming out of the movie theater talking about the film and after a small disagreement about a scene NiChia punched her in the face. She never said anything about her and NiChia arguing back and forth, or the fact that she participated in the fight as well. Shanice only made it seem like NiChia was beating her up, while she lied on the ground begging her to stop. Dominique tried to interrupt and tell what really happened, but each time, the officer told her to keep her mouth shut. She was so mad that she wanted to beat Shanice's ass herself. Wanting to prove her point, she walked around the parking lot searching for one of the people who recorded the fight, but couldn't find anyone. What she didn't know was that once they saw the police, they went on about their business.

While Shanice continued to fabricate the story, Dominique got in her car and explained to her sister what was going on. She told NiChia about all of the things that Shanice was saying and how she thought that she might go to jail behind it. NiChia had already known that something wasn't right when she saw Shanice standing by her car acting like she was so damn hurt. She knew that she had beaten her ass, but there was no reason for her to be acting like she couldn't even stand up, when she was doing just fine before the police showed up. Even before she started her performance, NiChia already knew that she was headed to jail because of how Shanice looked. Although Dominique thought her friend wasn't going to say anything, NiChia was certain that she would. Shanice would never have allowed her to get away with beating her up the way she had. Jail was in her future and she knew it. It wasn't her first time getting in trouble for fighting, so she was prepared for it.

Just as Dominique was climbing out of her car, she looked up and saw the police officers approaching. They immediately walked over to the passenger side where NiChia was seated and ordered her to step out of the car. Once she did, they told her to put her hands behind her back because she was under arrest for *Aggravated Battery on a Pregnant Female*. Both NiChia and Dominique looked at each other with wide eyes because neither of them knew anything about Shanice being pregnant. She hadn't even mentioned anything about it all, even during the fight. Just then, an ambulance pulled into the parking lot before it stopped directly beside the patrol car. The larger officer continued to cuff NiChia, while the other went over to where the ambulance was.

Dominique marched back over to Shanice, who was now being tended to by the EMS workers. Before she made it there, she was stopped by the skinny officer and told to go back to her vehicle. She tried to explain that Shanice was her best friend, but he wasn't trying to hear it. Since she wasn't able to talk to Shanice, she asked him where NiChia was being taken and was told that she was going to the Clayton County Jail. Feeling both angry and defeated, Dominique did as she was told. She climbed into her car and pulled out the parking lot. As soon as she hit the freeway, she sped the entire way home.

"Damn, I'm glad to see that I wasn't dying!" Dominique yelled as soon she Deondre stepped in the door.

"What you tripping about now?" Deondre asked, even though he knew exactly why she was mad.

He had spent the last hour checking on Shanice. She called him as she was being transported to the hospital after the fight. When he first saw her face, he was mad as hell and wanted to beat NiChia's ass himself. She had done a number on Shanice. Both of her eyes were black, her nose was broken, and her face was covered with bruises. Even her back had been scarred up from when she was drug across the pavement by her hair. Deondre knew that those marks would heal. He was more concerned about the baby. Although he wasn't happy about the fact that Shanice was pregnant again, she was still carrying his child. He would have still been there had Shanice's mother not have been on her way. With her knowing that he was with Dominique, it would have looked odd with him being there without her.

"I've called your phone about a hundred times, and yo' ass ain't even bother to answer." She stood up from the couch. "What if something was wrong with either me or DJ?"

He looked down at her with his face blank of emotion and asked, "Is something wrong?"

"No, but that's not the fucking point! The point is that I've been calling you!"

"Look man, my phone died," he lied.

"What the fuck ever!" Dominique screamed before turning around and walking into the kitchen. Her throat was dry and she needed something to drink.

Deondre kicked off his shoes and went towards the kitchen as well. "If you called that many times, you must have wanted something. What was it?"

"I need a thousand dollars to get Peanut outta jail,"

she told him, twisting off the top of the bottle of water and taking a swig.

"Why the hell is she in jail?" he asked, as if he didn't already know.

Dominique went on to explain everything that had happed from the time that she, NiChia, and Shanice had all got together, to the end of the fight. She told Deondre about how she thought everything was going well, until Shanice started to egg NiChia on, even before they got inside the movies. The entire time she talked, Deondre listened, but he already knew that he wasn't giving her any money to get NiChia out of jail. He couldn't stand her, and Dominique already knew it. NiChia was loud, with a smart ass mouth, and always trying to fight. Deondre was looking forward to the day that somebody beat her ass. He was salty that it hadn't been Shanice.

"It's crazy because Peanut didn't even know that Nicy was pregnant, so why is she being charged with it. Hell, I didn't even know." Dominique shook her head. "Anyways, I was told that her bond was ten thousand dollars, but if I get a bondsman, she can get out with just a thousand, Dominique told him, once she finished with the story.

"She ain't got no money?" Deondre asked, knowing that she didn't.

NiChia worked as a nail tech not far from where she lived. She mind decent money, but it wasn't like she was balling. What she did make went towards helping their grandmother, clothes, and other things she may have wanted.

Dominique looked at him like he was crazy. "I don't know if she had money or not. I'm asking you."

"Well, I ain't giving you no money to get her out. She should've thought about that before she started fighting."

"Tell me you playing." When he didn't say anything, Dominique stared at Deondre in disbelief. "I can't believe that you gone sit here and tell me that I can't have no money to get my sister out because *she should've thought about that before she started fighting*," she mocked him, before taking a step back and putting her hand on her hip. "You must have lost yo' damn mind! That's my fucking family that's locked in that jail, and you want me to leave her there. Fuck you, Dre!" Dominique grabbed her water, tossed it in the trash, and walked out of the kitchen.

"Wait!" Deondre yelled as he followed after her. "So you mad at me because I won't pay somebody else's bond *after* she beat the hell out of *your* best friend?"

"Not somebody. My fucking sister!" Dominique yelled over her shoulder. She walked into the living room and snatched up her purse. "And don't you worry about whose ass she beat. You know what, you have really been feeling yo'self lately."

"I ain't feeling shit," Deondre told her, watching her walk towards the front door.

"Whatever, Dre. I'm sure it's some funky ass bitch that's pumping yo' head up," she snapped.

"Ain't no bit—"

"Whatever the reason, you better get it together before you fuck around and be sorry," Dominique interrupted. "Then you wonder why I didn't want to get married right away, and it's because of shit like this. Maybe I should rethink the whole fucking thing!" With that, she walked out of her door, slamming it behind her.

Deondre stood there with a dumb look on his face. He knew that Dominique would be mad, but didn't think that she would be so upset that she'd be threatening to not marry him. They had talked about the argument they'd had not too long ago, and she explained that she didn't want to rush into things because he had so much going on at that time. Never did she mention not wanting to do it because of the bullshit that she thought he was doing. Hearing it now made Deondre wonder if she planned to marry him at all, or was she just stringing him along. He started to run out of the house after her and tell her that he'd give her the money, but his pride wouldn't let him. What Dominique said hurt his feelings, and he'd be damn if he ran after her to kiss her ass. At that moment, she needed him, not the other way around.

Outside, Dominique sat inside her car heated. She couldn't believe that Deondre was acting the way he was. He had never had a problem giving her money before, no matter what the issue was, so why was he tripping now. It was no secret that Deondre didn't like NiChia because the feeling was mutual. She didn't like his ass either. She said that it was because he was an opportunist. NiChia believed that the only reason why Dominique was with him was because of the fact that he helped her when she was down and out. She made it known on more than one occasion that that was how she felt and because of it, Deondre couldn't stand her. Dominique knew that before she asked him for money, but never thought that he would deny helping her sister out because of their issues. NiChia was her family and whether he liked it or not, if they got married, she would be his as well.

Dominique started her car and backed out of her driveway. She was headed back to McDonough to her grandmother's house. DJ was with still here, and Dominique missed her baby. As she drove down the street, she wondered what Franny would say once she found out that NiChia had been arrested yet again. Dominique knew that she would be upset because the last time she'd gotten in trouble, Franny had to be the one to bail her out. Of course, NiChia paid her back, but Franny said that wasn't the point. She wanted her granddaughter to stop using her fist to settle things because she was afraid that one day she was going to run into somebody who would hurt her. Dominique dreaded telling her grandmother the news and wished that she had to money to get her out before Franny found out.

A lightbulb went off in Dominique's head when she thought of somebody that she knew would help her. She pulled into the first gas station she saw, parked, and grabbed her cell phone from her purse.

"Hello," Kaleb answered.

"What you doing?" she asked with a smile on her face. Just hearing his voice made her feel better.

"Nothing, just sitting here. What you up to?"

"Nothing much," Dominique replied. "I need a favor."

"What you need?" Kaleb asked, wondering what it was that she needed. Dominique never asked him for anything, so he knew that it had to be important.

"Peanut got locked up, and I need to bail her out."

"How much you need?" he inquired.

It didn't matter how much she said she needed, Kaleb already had plans to give it to her. Not only would he do it for Dominique, but for NiChia as well. They had gotten closer since she and Desmond had been kicking it and to Kaleb, she was good people. She was crazy as hell, but cool.

"Her bond is ten thousand, but they said that if I get

a bondsman, she can get out with a thousand dollars."

"Don't worry about getting a bondsman," he told her. "I'll give you the whole ten."

"No Kaleb, you don't have to do that. The thousand is more than enough," Dominique told him truthfully. "I don't mind going through the bondsman. I just want to get her out of there."

"I said I got you," Kaleb insisted. "I'll pay her bond, and I'm sure that Des will take care of getting her a good lawyer. You know my nigga all in love and shit," he joked.

"I know he is. Shit, Peanut is too. They just be faking." Dominique laughed. "You know what I just realized?"

"What?"

"That you never even asked me what she did to go to jail."

"There was no need," Kaleb divulged. "She's your sister, and that's all that matters."

As soon as he said that, Dominique's heart melted. Although she wanted to be happy, she couldn't help but to feel a little sad. There she was talking to her friend, who was also the guy she was creeping with, and he didn't hesitate to give her what she asked for, no matter what the reason was; while her fiancé just flat out told her no. Deondre didn't care that although NiChia had violently beaten her best friend down, Shanice was the one who started. Even that didn't matter. He should have just had her back just because.

"What am I going to do with you?" Dominique asked not just to him, but to herself as well.

"Hopefully, you can love me again," Kaleb replied.

Dominique was about to say something in response, when she heard someone speaking in the background.

"Baby, I'm about to go shopping. I'll be back in a few hours. I'll call you when I'm on my way, so you can get dressed to go snorkeling," a female voice spoke.

"Alright, be careful." Kaleb yelled. "Hello."

"Yeah," Dominique answered in a dry tone.

"Now, what were you saying?"

"Nothing."

"What's wrong with you?" he asked when he noticed that it sounded as if she had an attitude.

Dominique smacked her lips. "Why you ain't tell me that you were with her?"

"I didn't think it mattered. Besides, I answered the

phone for you when you called, so apparently you were more important," Kaleb told her, not understanding what her issue was.

"Whatever Kaleb. Where are you anyway?"

"What?"

"I asked where you were. You can't be here if you're going snorkeling."

Kaleb thought for a minute before he answered, "I'm in the Virgin Islands."

Dominique snorted. "You gotta be kidding me."

"What?"

Although she heard him, Dominique didn't answer because she was too upset. It was no secret that Kaleb was involved with someone. He had told her all about his relationship with Tiera the day they met up at the park. Even though she and Kaleb were only friends at the time, Dominique still felt some kind of way after hearing about it. It was something about finding out that he was involved with someone else that got under her skin. Dominique knew that she was wrong for expecting Kaleb not to have moved on, even though she had. That still didn't stop her from being mad.

Dominique felt something wet drop on her hand.

When she lifted it up and wiped it across her face, she realized that she was crying. It was then that she accepted the fact that she cared way more than she put on. It killed her to know that Kaleb was off having fun with another woman. The mere thought of him touching someone else the way that he touched her only a few days prior, had her sick. The way he kissed her, the way he moaned her name when he was just about to cum. *How could he profess to love me so much when he clearly loves her?* Dominique couldn't understand what Kaleb was trying to do. *Is this all a fucking game?*

"You know what, never mind. I'll find another way to get the money," she spoke.

"What? Why?" Kaleb was confused.

"Don't worry about it. I'll find a way," Dominique told him, not really knowing if she could.

"I don't understand you, Nikki. It's not like I lied to you. You knew all about Tiera from the very beginning, so why you tripping? I just don't get it. You're mad at me because I'm with my girl, when you got a man...better yet, a fiancé," Kaleb scoffed. "I've tried to get you to leave him and be with me, but you always give me excuse after excuse. It's like you want me to just sit around and wait until you make up your mind about who you want. Is that it?" he asked. "If not, what exactly is it that you want from me?"

"You want to know what it is that I want from you, Kaleb?"

"Yes, I do—"

"I want you to leave me the fuck alone and lose my number!" Dominique yelled, cutting him off. Before he got a chance to say another word, she disconnected the call and threw her phone into the passenger seat. "Ugh!" she screamed out in frustration.

The rims of her eyes continued to fill with tears and before she knew it, she was bawling. Her shoulders shook violently as she cried hard. Dominique knew that she didn't really want what she had said to Kaleb, she was just mad. She was mad that he was with someone else. She was mad at how nonchalant he was about it and most of all, she was mad at herself for falling so hard for him once again. In the little time that they had been messing around, things had gotten hectic. She realized that she was playing a dangerous game, one that could destroy the family that meant so much to her. Dominique pulled down her visor and opened the attached mirror. When she saw that her eyes were red and puffy, she felt even worse. There she was crying over a man who was about to go snorkeling with another woman, as if he didn't have a care in the world.

"Get it together, bitch," Dominique sniffled. "Get it together."

After wiping the tears away from her face, she came to a conclusion. She was going to work on her relationship with Deondre. Dominique realized that while she was accusing him of cheating, she was doing the same thing. She wasn't sure if he really was stepping out on her, or if it was her guilty mind that made her think that he was. Dominique was aware of what she had to do about her Kaleb situation. The only way that she could move on with her life was to let him go, no matter how bad it would hurt. The problem was it easier said than done.

Chapter Seventeen

Shanice examined her face for the hundredth time that day. It had been almost two weeks since her fight with NiChia, and her bruises were all healed, all except for her broken nose. It was still a little swollen and hurt like hell sometimes, but her doctor explained that that would all go back to normal in just a few more weeks. Shanice couldn't wait until that happened because she was tired of worrying about it. She remembered the punch that caused her nose to break. The cracking sound was something that she would never forget. It hurt so bad, and there was so much blood. Just the thought of it caused Shanice to cringe. Her nose being broken was not even all of her injuries. She walked away from that fight with two black eyes, bruises on her face and back, as well as chunks of her hair pulled out. It was so bad that she was forced to give up her sew-ins and trade them in for a wig, for the time being.

Just thinking about the entire thing had Shanice mad all over again. She was glad that NiChia had gotten arrested and charged with attacking her the way she did. That's exactly what the bitch deserved. Shanice was already going to go to the police station to press charges after the fight, so when the patrol car pulled into the parking lot, it actually saved her the gas, as well as the time. She laughed when she remembered how much of a show she put on in front of the officers. You would have thought that she was really afraid for her life. She did such a good job that she was giving a temporary restraining order against NiChia. She would have to stay at least a thousand feet away from her, wherever she was at. *No more girls' days I suppose,* she snickered to herself. It wasn't that she really liked them anyway and Dominique knew that.

Dominique knew just how much she and NiChia hated each other, but she always found a way to try to get them together. It was like she liked to see them argue. Then once they got started, she would try to calm them both down, like that was what she really wanted. Their fight was just as much her fault as it was NiChia's. She knew what kind of person her sister was. Shit, everyone around them knew, that's why no one wanted to deal with her. It was no secret that NiChia was a ghetto, shit talking, live wire, who fought damn near everyone she came in contact with. She always used the excuse that she got it from her mother, but that was exactly what it was, an excuse. NiChia fought because it was what she liked to do. Unfortunately for her, this time she was going to pay because Shanice had no plans on letting her get away with what she did.

Shanice laughed when she thought about the stupid look on her face when the police officer placed the handcuffs on her. It was comical. She looked like a scared little girl, instead of the *Billy Badass* she thought she was minutes prior. She thought she was big shit while she was dragging her all around the parking lot by her hair because she had a bunch of spectators watching. Shanice thought about the fact that she had yet to run across the video of the fight and hoped like hell that whoever recorded it kept it to themselves. It was embarrassing to say the least, and she didn't want anyone seeing it that didn't have to. She wondered if it did come up, if it could be used as evidence to prosecute NiChia all the way. Since she plead not guilty and was out on bond, Shanice didn't know how the case would end. She hoped that she would get jail time because that was exactly what she deserved.

"How is your nose feeling, Nicy?" her mother asked as she walked into her bedroom.

Even though Shanice had moved into her own apartment, she still had a place to sleep when she came over to visit her parents. Even London had her own room, which was filled with every single toy her little heart desired. Mr. and Mrs. Wilson loved to spoil their granddaughter, just as they'd spoiled Shanice. Although she was now grown, they still did everything they could to make sure that she didn't want for anything. With her father, Omar, being a truck driver and away most of the time, he always tried to compensate his absence by giving his daughter everything she wanted and more. Her mother, Mya, who was an elementary school teacher, did the same. What neither of them didn't realize was that they were creating a monster. They let Shanice get away with everything because in their eyes, she could do no wrong.

"It's feeling a little better. The doctor said that it should be like new in a few weeks," Shanice replied as she relayed her doctor's message.

"Well, I know you'll be glad. I still can't believe that damn girl did you like that," Mrs. Wilson said. When she got the call from her daughter telling her what happened, she was livid. She rushed to the hospital to check on her. "I'm just happy that the baby is alright."

"Me too." Shanice smiled, tucking a piece of her hair behind her ear. "I was so worried."

Mrs. Wilson walked over to her daughter. "I know you were baby," she told her, placing her hand on her shoulder. "Have you talked to Lamar yet?"

"Yeah, he's glad that the baby is okay too, ma."

"Baby, are we ever going to meet this guy?" her mother asked. "You guys have been together for almost four years, are expecting your second child, and your father and I still haven't met him. Is there something you want to tell me?"

"What do you mean?"

"Just what I said. Why haven't you brought him around to meet us yet?"

Shanice was getting annoyed. She was tired of her mother and everybody else asking her about her baby daddy. It was her business and not theirs. Even though her parents bought London everything and then some, she never asked them for anything for her child because Deondre took care of his daughter. He made sure that she had everything she needed, plus more. He may not be around daily, but he always did his part. Who London's father was wasn't any of her mother's concern. She wanted to tell her that, but held her tongue because she knew better.

"Jesus ma, not this again," Shanice sighed. "How come we have to have this conversation every time I come over here?"

"Because I want to know what the hell is going on, Shanice!" Mrs. Wilson raised her voice. She had never really yelled at her daughter before, so Shanice knew that she had to be mad, that and the fact that she called her by her full first name. "You come in here and tell me that you're pregnant for the second time by some guy that I haven't even met for the first time. Is this man married or something...is that why you are hiding him?"

"No ma, he's not married."

"Well, what is it? You are keeping him a secret for a reason, and I want to know what it is!" When her mother walked around and stood directly in front of her with her hands on her hips, Shanice knew she was serious. "I'm not leaving this room until you tell me something."

"London—"

"She's napping, so I got plenty of time."

"It's complicated."

Mrs. Wilson reached back and pulled up Shanice's vanity chair and took a seat.

"Well, un-complicate it."

Taking a deep breath, Shanice couldn't believe that she was about to finally tell her mother the truth. She started to make up a lie, but didn't have the energy to do so. She was tired; tired of all of the secrecy, the lying, and sneaking around. Shanice knew that even after she told her mother her secret, nothing would change. Her mother may have liked Dominique, but she was her child and right or wrong, she always had her back.

"It's Dre," she whispered.

"Dre who?" her mother asked with her eyes almost popping out of her head. She knew that her daughter wasn't talking about who she thought she was talking about.

"Deondre."

"Oh my God, Shanice! No, not Nikki's boyfriend," Mrs. Wilson squealed. "Please tell me that that's not who you're talking about." When Shanice dropped her head, she knew that was exactly who she was referring to.

"Is that why her sister fought you?"

"No, that had nothing to do with our fight."

Mrs. Wilson raised her eyebrows before she asked, "Are you sure?"

"Yes mother."

"Why would you do that to your best friend?"

"I liked him first!" Shanice yelled. "I liked him since I was younger, and she knew that," she lied. "She didn't care, so why would I?"

"You may have liked him baby, but they had a child together."

"I had one first," Shanice pouted. She was mad that her mother was taking Dominique's side. "London is older than DJ," she said, trying to prove her point.

"Nicy, baby..."

Mrs. Wilson dropped her head in her hands. She was trying to wrap her head around what her daughter had just told her. All this time she and her husband thought that Shanice's child's father was some married man. Never in a million years did they think that it would have been someone who had been around for years. Deondre was like family to them, as was Dominique, so to hear that news was definitely a shocker. Mrs. Wilson continued to sit there quiet. She was trying to find the right words to say, but nothing came to her. She was disappointed in her daughter at that moment because Shanice knew better.

"I'm so lost right now," she said honestly, "and I'm trying to figure out where I went wrong. Your father and I have tried our best to lead by example. We've been married since way before you were born. Us being together in the same household is all you know. Still, you end up being some man's mistress."

"I'm not his mistress."

"What do you call it?" When Shanice didn't say anything, she continued. "Exactly. You can say what you want out of your mouth, but that's exactly what you are. You just told me that London was born first right?"

"Yeah," Shanice replied.

"So, if that was the case, why didn't he settle down and be with you? Why is he with Dominique?"

"I don't know, ma," she answered truthfully.

Shanice never really knew why Deondre had never left Dominique. When she would ask him about it, he would just skip over the question and move on to something else. Most of the time he would find a way to argue, and she would forget about it all together.

"It's because he's using you, baby." Mrs. Wilson gave her daughter the truth. She was tired of sugar coating things for her. Today she would get a lesson; a lesson that she hoped her child would stick to. "You have two choices. Either he leaves her and be with you, or you leave him alone for good."

"Ma-"

"Ma my ass!" she yelled. "I'll be damned if my daughter continues to be some negro's side piece. He put a ring on her finger, while you're popping out his damn babies. He's at home playing daddy to his son. What about London, Shanice?"

"London is well taking care of," Shanice responded, taking up for Deondre. "He makes sure that she has everything she needs."

"Besides a daddy," her mother pointed out. "That baby doesn't even know who her daddy is. She can't because it would be too dangerous for her to know. Might mess up what y'all got going. Well, that is no longer happening, so you better give him an ultimatum."

"You can't tell me—"

"I can, and I will. Do it, or stay away from here," Mrs. Wilson demanded. "We didn't raise you this way, and I'm not going to stand by and allow you to keep playing the fool."

Shanice didn't say anything, as he mother got up and pushed her chair back in. She was confused by what had just happened. Her mother was telling her that either Deondre leaves Dominique and be with her, or she can't be with him anymore. If she decided to continue to creep with him, her mother was basically washing her hands with her. As she watched her mother walk past her and out of her bedroom door without even looking back, she was torn. There was no doubt that she was serious about what she said. Shanice loved Deondre so much, but she also loved her parents. She couldn't picture her life without either of them, but there was a decision to be made. Either she had to do what her mother had instructed, or cut them out of her life.

Shanice wondered what Deondre would do if she gave him the ultimatum. Would he leave Dominique and they become a couple, or would he walk away from her and their children? That was something that she really wanted to know, even though she couldn't bear the thought of the latter. Shanice's mind began to work in overdrive. She started to think of things she could do to put a wedge between Dominique and Deondre. Although she had been trying to do that all along, she knew that she had step it up for him to walk away for good. Shanice knew that whatever it was, it had to be something very serious. She decided to focus her attention on Dominique, who had, for the past month or so, been acting distant towards her.

Her phone calls had all but stopped, and she had been spending quite a bit of time at her grandmother's house, which was something that she hadn't done since she'd been with Deondre. Everyone who knew Dominique knew that she hated to drive, so it was something important that kept her making the hour trip every weekend. Shanice speculated that it had something to do with Kaleb. Although she hadn't seen the two together, she knew for a fact that NiChia was kicking it with Desmond, and since he was Kaleb's best friend, it would only make sense. An evil grin spread across Shanice's face when she thought about what Deondre would do if he found out that Dominique was in fact been dealing with her ex.

Just like that, Shanice felt better. She didn't have solid proof about her accusations, but she was going to damn sure find out. There was no way that she was going to lose the man that she loved because she had worked too hard and sacrificed too much to give up now. Her mother was right about one thing and that was that she wasn't going to continue to be someone's side piece. Shanice vowed to win over Deondre's heart, even if she had to throw her best friend under the bus. Dominique didn't deserve him in the first place. She also didn't deserve the life that she thought she was about to live. It was no secret that Deondre was about to do big things, and Shanice planned to be the one on his arm when he did. No one, including Dominique, was going to stand in her way.

Chapter Eighteen

"Why can't I leave you alone?" Dominique asked as she sat on top of Kaleb, breathing hard.

He licked his lips and smiled. "Because you love me just as much as I love you," he responded.

Dominique couldn't do anything but sit there quietly. She hated to admit it, but he was right. She was able to stay away from Kaleb for a little over a week. She was miserable the entire time, and knew that he was too because every time she turned around, he was blowing up her phone. He called so much the first few days that she had to put her phone on *Do Not Disturb* mode when Deondre was home, so that he wouldn't get suspicious. Dominique was surprised that Deondre hadn't asked her about what she had been up to because lately, she was never home. If may have been because he was up to no good himself, but Dominique couldn't say because she hadn't really being paying him attention anyway. Her mind and body was too preoccupied with Kaleb to even care.

After Dominique sat down and really thought about it, she knew that she was wrong to punish Kaleb for having a girlfriend, no matter how much it hurt her. He was right when he basically said that the ball was in her court. It was her who was holding them up as a couple, not him, so who was she to get mad about what he chose to do, when she was doing the same thing? Dominique made the decision to continue to deal with Kaleb and see how things went. She still wasn't thrilled to know that he was with someone else, but she would try her best to understand his situation the same way that he understood hers. The next time that he called her, she answered. All it took was her to hear his voice, and she was sucked right back in. That very same day, she packed her an overnight bag and drove up to her grandmother's house to drop DJ off. Even though she knew that he was too young to understand what was going on, she still thought it was disrespectful, and whenever she was with Kaleb, she didn't have her son.

That day, Deondre claimed that he was going to New Orleans for a few days, so he wasn't there to question her about where she was going, which was a good thing because Dominique didn't have it in her to lie. All she wanted at that time was to get to Kaleb because she missed him so much. It just so happened that his girl was out of town as well for her job. Since they both didn't have to answer to anyone, they took advantage of their freedom.

"We have to figure out something," she told him, climbing off of him and kissing him once on the lips.

They were at another one of Kaleb's properties. They had just finished getting hot and heavy, and Kaleb was exhausted. He gripped Dominique's waist and pulled her body closer towards him. She responded by draping her arm across him stomach and laying her head on top of his chest. Kaleb inhaled and smelled the fruity fragrance of her hair.

Kaleb brought her head up to look her in the eyes. "Figure out what?"

"Us. What are we going to do about us? Are you we going to just keep creeping around?"

"You already know what I want," he told her seriously. "I want you to be mine. I don't say anything or push the issue, but I hate it when you leave me and go back home to him. That shit hurts, but I accept it because I know that's ya man, and the father of your child."

"I know, I feel the same way when I think about you being with her." Dominique hesitated for a moment, before she asked, "Do you love her?"

Kaleb though about her question for a minute before he replied, "Yes, I love her, but not the way that I love you."

"What does that mean?"

Although she tried to stop them, Dominique's eyes pooled with tears. When one fell, Kaleb brushed it away with his finger. He used his hand to tilt her chin upwards while he looked down at her intently. He wanted to make sure that she completely understood what he was about to say.

"I love Tiera. I care about her, and I would never want to see her hurt, but I'm not in love with her. You are who my heart belongs to, always has and probably always will. I remember the first time I saw you again,"

Kaleb told her, thinking back to the day that she walked into the house with her dude. "It was as if time stood still. I was shocked, sad, happy, and confused all at once. I didn't know whether to speak or act like I didn't know you." He laughed. "I think I played it cool though, what do you think?"

Dominique smiled. "You did a good job at first. Then you got thirsty."

"I'll take that." Kaleb laughed again. "I was happy as hell to see you. You don't know how much I missed you and now that I got you back, I don't plan on letting you go again." He leaned down and slipped his tongue into her mouth. Dominique allowed him to kiss her deeply, while she rolled onto her back and opened her legs. She was ready for round two and by the looks of things, he was too.

"I saw the way you were lusting all over the screen in there, and I'm a little hurt." Kaleb pretended to wipe imaginary tears from his eyes. "I can't believe you were mentally cheating on me.

"Shut up boy, you know Denzel and Mark Wahlberg are both my men." Dominique laughed, smacking him on the arm. "I told you that before we went in.

They had just come from watching the new movie, *2 Guns*. The entire time that the film was playing, Dominique couldn't keep her eyes off of the screen. It was not only filled with action, but it was also unpredictable. She couldn't deny that she really enjoyed the movie and loved the fact that both her men crushes had major roles in the film. After they exited the theater, she and Kaleb walked hand and hand over to his truck. It felt good to be out and about with him, without having to worry about being scene. Not only was Deondre out of the state, but they were an hour from where she lived, so she was sure that they wouldn't run into anyone who knew them.

When Kaleb opened her door, she climbed inside and put on her seat belt. That was yet another thing that he and Deondre were different about. Dominique couldn't remember one time, other than the day she came home from the hospital with DJ, that Deondre had ever opened her door for her. They usually just climbed in at the same time and headed to their destination. Once Kaleb got around to the driver's side and climbed in, Dominique was smiling.

"What?" He looked at her, wondering why she was cheesing so hard.

"Nothing, it's just funny to see how much you've grown from the person you used to be," she told him. "You were such a hot head. I remember you and Des used to always get in trouble for fighting. I'm glad that you both have changed."

"Yeah, me too. Of course, Des is still a little rough around the edges, but he's doing a lot better." Kaleb nodded his head. "Hopefully some of his laid back mannerisms will rub off on Peanut's crazy ass. That girl is a nut!"

"You ain't lying about that," Dominique agreed. "She told me that she's trying to chance her ways. Going to jail after that shit with Shanice spooked her, I think, because it wasn't just an assault charge because there was a baby involved," she explained. "You know Nicy hasn't called me since the fight. Hell, I didn't even know the bitch was pregnant."

"Hmph, I wouldn't even worry about her grimy ass."

Dominique sat up in her seat and looked in his direction, "Why you say that?"

"Don't worry about, it's nothing. Anyway, you staying with me tonight?" Kaleb asked, changing the subject.

"Yeah, but I didn't bring anything to wear. I was supposed to go back home later today. I guess I can go to my grandmother's and see if I have something over there."

"Nah, I have something better in mind. Southlake Mall is only around the corner, we'll go grab you something.

"Sounds good," Dominique responded, as they pulled out of the parking lot headed.

Inside the mall, they stopped and grabbed them some Chinese food from one of the restaurants in the food court. As they ate, they talked about their plans for the evening. Dominique brought up grabbing a few DVD's from *RedBox* and calling to see if NiChia and Desmond wanted to come over and make it a movie night. She hadn't been spending much time with her sister because they were both so preoccupied with the new men in their lives, and figured that she could kill two birds with one stone. Kaleb agreed that it was a good idea and said that he would grab a few bottles of liquor before they headed back.

Once they were finished eating, they headed over to *Finish Line,* where Kaleb purchased them both a few pairs of shoes. There next stop was to *Children's Place,* where Dominique started to grab a few cute things for DJ. When they made it to the register to pay, Kaleb pulled out his credit card and prepared to swipe it, but Dominique stopped him. She explained that she didn't feel comfortable allowing him to pay for clothes for her son. Kaleb understood what she was coming from, but let her know that even though he hadn't met DJ personally, he loved him just as much as he loved her, so he didn't mind buying him things. Still, Dominique paid for them herself, and they left the store.

"What do you think of this?" Dominique asked, holding a lotion bottle up to his nose.

"I don't like it," he told her, making a face. "It smells a little too fruity to me."

"I thought so too," she agreed. "Let me go over here and see what else they have."

While Dominique went over to the other wall of

fragrances that lined *Victoria Secret*, Kaleb leaned against the wall. In his hands, he held their shoes, as well as everything that they had picked up along the way. He watched as she picked up bottle after bottle, putting each of them to her nose. Some caused her to shake her head, while others were placed in the bag that an employee had given her upon walking in. Once Dominique had found everything that she was looking for, she walked back over to them with a smile on her face. Kaleb stared at her lovely face because she was so beautiful.

"You ready to go?" she asked. "I got a few more. They had a different kind of Vanilla than I got, so I grabbed that one. It smells so good." Dominique held her hand out so he could sniff it.

"I like it and can't wait to get a closer smell of it," he told her with a sneaky grin.

She smacked her lips and rolled her eyes. "You so damn nasty."

"You like it."

Together, they went over to the line. There were a few people ahead of them, so they made small talk while they waited. Dominique giggled as Kaleb whispered nasty things in her ear. She couldn't wait to model all of the sexy panty and bra sets that she had picked up for him later that night. She had already called Franny and told her that she wasn't going to come and pick up DJ until the following morning, and just like she expected, her grandmother didn't care. She loved keeping her great grandson. He reminded her of Jessie when he was a little boy. With no other kids in the house, he kept her busy and that was just what she needed.

They continued to talk while the cashier rang up everything that they had placed on top of the counter. As the number kept going up higher and higher, Dominique began to feel uneasy with the amount of money that she was spending. Kaleb noticed her apprehension and pulled her closer to him, before he let her know that it was alright. Other than the bond money for NiChia, Dominique had never asked him for nothing, so he didn't mind spending his money on her. The truth of the matter was, she could have asked him for anything because what he really wanted to do was give her the world. Kaleb told her exactly that, which lead her to grab his face and pull him in for a deep kiss.

Once she let him go, he paid for her things and she grabbed her bags. When they turned around to walk away, Dominique smile turned into a look of shock, as she froze in her tracks. Since Kaleb wasn't paying any attention, he kept walking and he ran directly into the back of her. He was about to ask her what was wrong, when he looked up and saw what had had her shook. Standing right outside of the door was Deondre. The angry look on his face could not be mistaken. He glanced back and forth between Dominique and Kaleb, before he looked down and noticed all the bags they were carrying. Dominique was so scared that she didn't know what the hell she was going to do. *How much did he see? Did he catch the kiss I just gave Kaleb, or did he just walk up?* she thought to herself, as her mind raced. *What the hell am I going to do?*

Dominique prayed that Deondre didn't cause a scene in the store because she knew what he was capable of. She glanced over at Kaleb with shame because she knew that things were not going to go well. She hated to have drug him into her bullshit, but it was too late now. They had been caught.

"What the fuck you doing and where the hell is my

son?"

To Be Continued...

CPSIA information can be obtained
at www.ICGtesting.com
Printed in the USA
LVOW12s0904030416

481968LV00001B/126/P